D1519384

Love Devours
Tales of Monstrous Adoration

Also by Sarah Diemer

The Dark Wife
Sugar Moon

As Elora Bishop

Cage the Darlings
One Solstice Night
Crumbs: A Lesbian Hansel and Gretel
Braided: A Lesbian Rapunzel

With Jennifer Diemer

Sappho's Fables, Volume 1

LOVE DEVOURS

Tales of Monstrous Adoration

Sarah Diemer

For Jenn, always.

And for Tara:
Fellow monster sister.
Thank you for walking the halls of ink with me—
they shine because of your care and kindness.
I am deeply grateful.

CONTENTS

ACKNOWLEDGMENTS

As always, without the insight, awesome and kindness of Jennifer Adam, Tara Taylor and Bree Zimmerman, I would be lost. For my stories, their passion, attention to detail and extreme generosity knows no bounds. All of the good parts of these tales are directly linked back to the unerring support of these three phenomenal women. Any error left is mine alone. Thank you, from the bottom of my heart, for everything you do, guys—I am so grateful.

This volume of monstrous stories is dedicated to Tara Taylor, who has supported my writing, tales and words for longer and deeper than I can say. She is an irreplaceable bedrock in the foundation of my success, the knowledgeable, kind and trusted ear who listens to all of my crazy ideas, and the flawless pair of eyes that devours them and helps me see their seeds better. Tara, I adore you and am so grateful for your friendship. These monsters are for you. Thank you for being!

Thank you to Rachel Melcher for her unwavering love, strength and support. Thank you to Katelyn and Corey Verrill for their constant love and sharing of laughter. Madeline Claire Franklin is love, and Laura Diemer is courage and fire and strength. Thanks goes to my mom who always, *always* (somehow!) remembers every story idea and still gets excited about each new one. Thanks to Rhiannon Matich for the laughter, "that's what she said" moments and everything else, always. Laura Vasilion is as unwavering as a star with her support and love, and I am so grateful for it. Thanks to the good fairy for always seeing the good in me, and believing—I hope you know how much your friendship means to me.

Special thanks goes to the Moonjava Café, and Renee and Jeannine there…you ladies, your awesomeness and your glorious caffeine make all things possible.

My humblest love, gratitude and adoration goes to my wife, Jennifer Diemer. All that I am is because of you. I love you, baby.

I am continuously humbled and strengthened by the support and love shown to me by my fans. I can't begin to express (though I try!), what it means to me that you continue to tell me how much you love my stories, or how glad you are that they exist. All that I do is done for you. Thank you for receiving and supporting. You mean the world to me.

INTRODUCTION

I was born a monster.

That's what the protesters at the Pride Parade told me, anyway, bellowing into a megaphone while they held up a sign that announced "all gays go to hell."

My wife and I didn't even break stride as the protesters screamed. Instead, we kept marching, rainbow socks keeping a constant rhythm as we held up two signs between us. They announced to the world that on September 30, 2011, our church married us, *legally*.

The shouts of support drowned out the megaphone.

It's not the first time I've been called a monster. It won't be the last.

I was born gay. This is considered, by many, to be monstrous, which is, of course, the opposite of truth. But from the very beginning, I knew I was strange, different, so it's no surprise, of course, that I turned to the monsters of myth, of legend, of fairy tale, devouring their stories as their stories devoured me. Circe, condemning men to the shape of pigs. Medusa, once the most beautiful woman in

3

the world, now snake-headed and desperate. The harpies, throwing their necks back beneath the sharp sun, hooting with joy. These were wild women, fierce women, monstrous women, and as I paged through the old books, my eyes alight with a new fire, something began to burn in my belly, too.

Monsters were wild. Monsters were strong. Monsters were fierce and free.

If I was monstrous…perhaps it wasn't such a bad thing.

Monsters are my obsession, now, my heart well steeped in the old, dark stories, inventing new ones of my own. I dream of women with wings, women with sharp teeth and flashing eyes, women powerful and empowered and utterly monstrous.

And now I share them with you: monsters…reclaimed.

This book is for every girl and boy who has ever been called a monster. Every woman and man deemed monstrous for being different.

You are wild. You are strong. You are fierce and free.

All my love,

Sarah Diemer
August, 2012

4

F A R

One

Far was dead, and I could not live without her.

I bought her body with two coins and a kiss, paid for it like all of the other things on the dark markets--the monkey feet and star keys and lover brambles, bought and sold, pressed to palms in shadowed alleys, far away from the wandering gazes of the Gray Coats. The Robber I hired didn't say much when I kissed him, when I gave him the coins. He turned, and he disappeared into his warehouse, and I followed him and was sick along the inner wall, because the building smelled of death and ash and excrement. I almost lost him in the dark because of my retching, but I stumbled after, willing myself to keep pace with his long strides, anger driving me forward when nothing else could.

He pointed to a slump of burlap, vaguely human-shaped, and I peeled back the upper layer, saw her hair, her beautiful brown face, saw how it didn't look like her face anymore. I put down the cloth before I lost all I had left: my anger, my desire, my bitterness. I hefted her onto my shoulder and staggered under her weight and nearly tripped over another body on my way out of the nightmare.

In the dull glow of the city at night, I crept along

the alley and prayed to things I did not believe in to shield me, hide me from the Gray Coats, from the prowling beasts and birds that lined the roofs of buildings-- gargoyles and living monsters alike, watching the people below, hungry.

The shack wasn't a home; it wasn't even shelter from the citywide stench. But it had a door and a lock, and I was grateful to it for the first time in my life when I felt the solidity of wood and iron beneath my hands, shut out and bolted the city behind me, and set my burden down upon the floor as gently as I could. She seemed heavier than she'd been in life, unwieldy and stiff, and I wanted to be sick again when I peeled back the burlap and saw her not-face and realized all over again that I had lost her.

But I hadn't, I reminded myself, wiping my damp, shaking hands against my skirts, and raking them back through my disheveled mess of hair, thinking. My thoughts spun like swinging lanterns.

I had not lost her. She was here, in front of me. She'd only been dead for a single night. I might have enough time.

My hands were still shaking when I drew the circle in chalk on the floor, outlining her body in waves and points, writing out the words I remembered, the ones my hands knew when my mind did not: the language of the dead. I finished, and I sat back on my heels, touched her fingers with my own, winced at how cold she was.

I crossed the circle, put one boot on the inside, one on the out, and I felt the balance shift, felt the darkness draw close as a cloak, suffocating and heavy and almost comforting.

I stepped fully in, and everything was black.

It was quick, the change. Darkness, and then slight light, gray light. The shack and Far's body were gone, and the pair of stone lions stared down at me with their usual disdain as the wind blew from the yawning cave mouth, the entrance to After, and teased at my hair and face like rude children's fingers.

"After is closed to you," said one lion, unhinging its jaws, the sound of boulder against earth screeching into the stillness. "You are forbidden to this place, Mana."

I knelt, pressing my hands together, hoping the lions' eyesight was poor enough to overlook my fear. I was cunning. I had always been cunning. I could still be cunning.

"Oh, lords of After," I said quietly, bowing my head to them, eyes fixed to the dark earth, the shards of bone that stuck up through it like dead flower stalks. "I know that I am forbidden to this place."

"Then why have you come? Why have you returned, when we have warned you again and again that you enter After at your peril?" One lion lowered its massive head and affixed me with a granite gaze. I quaked and swallowed and felt the exhale of its breath between sharp and shining stone teeth.

"I lost something important here," I said, standing, never removing my eyes from the ground, my entire body tense. I had used so many ploys in the past to trick the lions, or confuse them, or flatter them, but now I had no heart for games. This was too important. "I come with an offering for you, that I may take a few heartbeats and retrieve what is precious to me. Surely you would not object to so short a dalliance through After? I will be gone before you can even blink your eyes."

"Surely you do not think us *stupid*," said the lion on the left, rather dryly. "First, you are forbidden, and second, why should we grant you any favor?"

"I would leave you my soul, until I return. If I do not return, it will be yours to keep." My voice was barely a whisper.

The lions looked to one another. The one on the right roared to the left, "A soul is a soul. She could not trick us in this."

They both stared at me together.

"Know that, if you deceive us, we will repay you in full, Mana, daughter of the city," said the one on the left, voice dangerous and soft, a rumbling purr. "We will hunt you over the city, and we will devour you whole. You will cease to be in all ways."

"Of course," I said too quickly, taking out a pin from my hair. "Here." And I pricked my thumb, sucking on the blood until it flowed fast, steady, and then I let it pool upon the ground, dripping out an amorphous shape upon the earth, over the bones. I let a hiss of pain escape as a lion pressed its paw to the dirt, sucked up my spirit through my blood until I felt faint enough to die, faint enough to waver, devoid of the courage to take another step.

"It is ours," said the lions, as one. "Go. Be quick. If you do not return in one thousand heartbeats, we will claim your soul forever."

I fell to my knees but stood, just as quickly, stumbling between their great shapes and through the cave into After.

I could find Far in one thousand heartbeats.

I would have to.

Darkness, the line of glowing souls, the density of earth overhead—the atmosphere of After never changed. Souls glimmered a sort of blue-white in the half light, like milk at midnight, standing one after the other in succession, beginning right at the gap and gateway of After and ending in the Recycler Chamber.

I raced along the line, looking at each face as the dead moved forward, step by slow step. They didn't notice me; they never did. It was so familiar, this sensation--my blood roaring through me as I tried to find the mark and tried not to get caught.

The Prehend's approach was silent as death, so

you had to watch for her. Just because I never got caught before didn't mean I wouldn't now. My skin crawled, and I kept glancing over my shoulder as I crept quickly along, between the rock wall and the shimmering spirits.

Please, Far--please still be here.

The Recycler Chamber glowed up ahead, a rounded room made of alabaster at the top of the hill. The line of souls fed up into it and disappeared inside. No soul ever came out of the Chamber. Rumor had it that the Chamber made a soul into someone new, so hopeful people got into the habit of calling it the Recycler.

I called it a curse. Who would trust their soul to a machine?

If Far had gone through the Chamber, I had already lost her.

I tripped as I turned a corner, tripped and put out my hand against the wall to steady myself. If I hadn't tripped, I might have missed her, might not have seen her flickering face. It was strange, how her face was duller than the others, how her whole body glowed less, but it made her easier to spot. She was there, standing there, and my heart leapt up, and I almost wept and cried out at once. Far, my Far, was still safe.

I stepped forward, placed my arms about her waist, pressed her to me and in me. I felt the familiar swell of my heart as a foreign soul entered and engulfed my insides, and I shook, euphoric with the sensation of housing another's essence within my body. Far did not think or move inside of me but remained still and quiet in my belly, and heavy, as if I'd eaten a too-full meal. I stood for a long moment, making certain she was secure, and I stepped back along the wall.

That was when I saw her.

The Prehend drifted along the line of spirits, shimmering in her own right, not blue but a deathly white, floating just above the ground. Her round black eyes were counting the dead, always counting the dead, and her mouth was closed, but I had seen her teeth from a distance before, knew how sharp they were, how full of them her mouth was. She moved sedately now, languid, as if in a dream, but if she saw me, pursued me, I would never be able to run fast enough to get away.

My heart pounded, and all my trickery left me. I didn't know what to do. She came from the direction of the gateway. She would have to catch me or pass me by, and she never passed *anyone* by.

I dropped to my knees and stopped breathing. I prayed and hoped the force of my prayer would be enough.

She slowed as she neared my crouching form, slowed to a crawl, and I saw the wisps of her garments twining with the souls as she mulled them over, as she ceased counting. She was too close to me, would surely see me, devour me. I knew it was over; everything was over.

But she moved on.

She kept drifting down the line, and I began to edge backward until I rounded the corner and scrabbled up from my hands and knees to take off at a flat run. My feet pounded against the dull hollow of the earth, and I ran from After like I had never run before.

My leg muscles burned with disuse, but my heart was elated. This was me, what I was--a Runner. I was the best at stealing back souls, or had been. Far had begged me to stop because my fellow Runners got…bad luck, failed to evade the Prehend, were devoured. Now there was only one other Runner left in all of the city, and he would never be as fast as me.

I burst out of the gap and stopped, gasping for breath between the two stone lions.

"Trouble?" asked the one on the right, malicious grin splitting its face.

I shook my head, held out my hand, and my blood

10

pooled up from the earth and flowed back into the tiny wound upon my finger. There were two souls in my body now, and they shifted and warred but eventually lay beside one another, curled round each other, at peace.

"No trouble at all," I whispered, and left After.

"Who did this to you?" I asked her, pressing my hand to her hand, to the wound in her palm that opened like a vicious smile across her skin.

"No one," she sighed, taking her fingers from me, pressing the wound to her shoulder to quell the flow of blood. "I did it to myself."

I tore at my hair, knelt down beside her, ready to weep or rage at her. I didn't know what to do. I never knew what to do with Far.

"It's all so messed up," she said, looking down at me with clear, deep eyes, so dark they reflected the light like mirrors. "It shouldn't be this way."

"What are you talking about?" Wary, I looked at the chinks in the shack's walls, the tiny holes where anyone could press an ear, hear her treasonous talk and, drag her away, lock her away, so that I'd never see her again. "Far, everything is fine…" I whispered, holding out my hands to her, my eyes begging: Please stop talking about this. Please don't talk about this.

"It's so fucked up." She backed away from me. "And you only add to it."

"I keep you safe," I said, pain lancing my heart. "I earn enough coin so that we don't have to worry, so that I can feed you, so that we can buy time."

"I don't want time," she whispered. "I want to be free."

I took her hand from her shoulder. She wept soundlessly. I poured unguents into the wound, and

11

together we watched the slash on her palm close, the flesh pouring into itself until the wound was gone—though, when I closed my eyes, I saw it still.

"Why won't you let me die?" she whispered to me, pillowing her head on my shoulder, and her tears traced familiar grooves along my chest. "Just let me fucking go."

I covered her lips with a finger, felt myself shaking.

Outside of the shack, stone claws scraped and clicked. The gargoyles began to hunt when the clock chimed twelve.

I pressed the herbs against her mouth and eyes and lay, bone weary, on the floor beside her. Far's soul had ported over to her body smoothly, but waking up was always difficult for the Reanima. This last step would either seal her back to the body or break the link, and if the link was broken, her soul would be lost to the city, to After…and to me.

I closed my eyes and prayed.

I never prayed to anyone specific. There were so many gods in the city, constructs born of overactive and desperate imaginations. But I suppose, in a sense, I prayed to ideas--the idea that she would wake up, that we could go back to the way things were. The idea that I had done the right thing in buying Far's body, fetching her soul, and willing her back to life, back to me.

She breathed in once, back arching up of a sudden, bending like a bow, and I leapt to my feet, terrified that, out of the hundreds of reanimations I had enabled, somehow I had botched this one--this most important, most precious one.

But she breathed in and out again, and her eyes

opened, milky, and she turned her head and looked up me.

"Mana?" she whispered, a growl low and deep in her throat. She coughed, coughed up blood, bile, and she said it again, my name. She said my name: "Mana?"

I gathered her into my arms, pressed her close to me, but she was pushing weakly against me, and she was crying out, saying my name over and over again--not in joy but in despair.

"Mana, what have you done?" she wailed, looking down at her hands, her blackened nails. Her wrists moved stiff as dolls' limbs. "You brought me back?"

"Shh," I whispered, pressing my finger to her lips; she slapped it away.

"I will not be quiet!" she raged and staggered to her feet--awkwardly, leaning against the wall of the shack, beating her breast with one loose fist. I stepped forward, held her arms to her sides, and she was as weak as a child, struggling and crying out.

"You've cursed me," she spat, and she pressed her face to my heart, and she gave in, then, sobbing against my breastbone, tearless. The Reanima could not weep.

I held her until she stopped, until--together--we knelt down upon the dirt floor once more. My heart pounded in my chest, knocking against my ribs as I listened closely to the world outside of our shack's four thin walls. I heard nothing; no one was coming. For now, in this moment, we were safe, both of us. Alive and safe.

"Why did you do this to me?" she hissed, her milky eyes red now, red and enlarged, and dazed looking. I stared at the floor, at my hands. I tried, but I could not look at her.

"I love you..." I began, but she was laughing and wailing and rocking, shaking her head as if I'd just said the funniest thing she had ever heard.

"If you loved me, you would have let *this* rot." She waved at her body, pounded her fists against her

13

thighs. "You would have let them bury me and be done with it."

"I *did* let them bury you," I whispered, but she was wailing again, and I couldn't let her wail; they would come for both of us if they heard her. I leaned forward, pressed my finger to her lips. It was a familiar gesture for both of us, but somehow it felt different now.

Far stopped, stopped sobbing and stared at me, and I looked into her eyes and felt myself falling away.

I had reanimated so many corpses. So many, I'd lost count. I was proud of it, my success as a Runner. I'd put souls back into bodies, reanimated them, and then let them go on and live out whatever life they had left in them, until they began to rot, until they could no longer hide from the world what they truly were. Their bodies eventually ran out of energy, like a broken machine, and then--where did the resurrected soul go when its mortal house crumbled? No one knew; no Runner knew. We just did what people asked of us, brought their dead ones back to them, restored lost life. Those who feared the Recycler, who mistrusted its purpose--well, we offered them another option. We offered them time.

But Far had waited all of her life to die. And I had stolen away her one wish.

"Why?" she whimpered, putting her face in her hands, and her hands on her knees. She crumpled before me, silent, piteous.

"I love you," I repeated, an explanation and apology in one.

"Don't you ever wonder what this is all about?" Far licked her fingers before grabbing another handful of taffy from the bag. "Where we come from, where we're going? Don't you think it's a little strange that none of us

14

knows?"

I shifted uncomfortably, held the bag out to her again, hoping the sticky candy would close her mouth for a little while. It was an uncharitable thought, but when she got into these moods and muttered treasonous words out loud--and in public, no less--my heart panicked. All it would take was one sentence overheard by one pair of ears. If Far got turned in to the Gray Coats, she would be gone fast as dreams, and I would lose her.

So I offered her more taffy.

"No, I mean, really," she said, twirling about a gravestone. "The Robbers dig up the bodies, and the Runners fetch souls and reanimate the bodies, but some souls go on to the Recycler, and where do they end up?

"One day we wake up here, and we have a place to live and some coins, and we're just expected to accept it all, to never wonder about what it means, or what could be...out there." Far pointed to the darkness surrounding the city. "This place doesn't even have a name."

"It's home," I told her, and pressed the bag of taffy into her hands. I had paid three coins for it, and the paper-wrapped pieces tasted of brackish water, but Far loved it, and I would do anything to make Far happy.

But Far was never happy.

"Don't you ever feel...trapped?" she whispered, dropping the bag onto a grave, gliding her fingers over my collarbones. I sighed, leaning against her hands.

"No, Far. I don't feel anything but love."

Her face twitched, and I saw how disappointed she was in my reply. In me. But I'd spoken the truth.

"We live our lives in this tiny place, in these tiny ways, and you never wonder why, or if there's more." Her words were dull, flat, but they entered my ears like sharp things. I shook my head, put my arms around her.

"You don't understand," I whispered, holding her close, squeezing her against me. "None of that matters."

"It matters very much, Mana," she said, but I stopped up her mouth with a kiss.

"Please eat," I begged her, holding out the bowl of rice, waggling it before her. Far stared down at the ground, as she had for hours, and did not acknowledge me, did not move, remained as silent as a statue, and as lifeless.

But she *had* life. I had given her life.

"Leave me," she whispered.

"No." My hand trembled, and I nearly dropped the bowl. I was afraid to leave her, was desperately afraid that somehow she would undo what I had done, slip free from her mortal coil, become an untethered soul and lost to me forever.

"Please eat," I whispered again, heart beating too fast. She pressed her face against the wall.

How long could this go on? How long could she refuse to nourish her body? How long would it function without food? In the beginning, the reanimated soul's ties to the physical were like spider silk, tenuous, and the connection had to be nurtured.

Far knew this. She knew, and she still refused to eat.

She was as stubborn as a Reanima as she had been in her first life, and I was going to lose her again.

Tryx knocked his special knock--three fast, three slow, two fast. The sound surprised me; I jumped, and the bowl clattered to the floor. Rice spattered my feet, Far's feet. She didn't stir. I got up and opened the door and ducked outside, let the holey panel of wood shut fast behind me.

"We need a Runner," Tryx said, leaning close.

"I can't. Ask Gand."

"Gand is gone."

We stared at one another for a very long moment.

"Gone," I repeated, and the word felt like lead on my tongue.

Tryx nodded. "Last night."

It might have been anything--Gand could have simply died, died in his bed, even--but I thought in that heartbeat of the Prehend and her promise to all Runners: torture first, and then the soul devoured, lost for all time. It's what we faced; it's why we were paid so well, and, really--in the city, our disgusting and dark little city--it was one guarantee in a haze of uncertainties.

"Will you do it?" asked Tryx.

If I Ran this last time, I would earn coin enough to buy food that would entice Far, food that she would be helpless to resist. I pushed my fingers through my hair, shut my eyes, breathed out the word before my brain could find reason to object. I said, "Yes."

"When the clock swings to six, at Baron's. You'll know the client when you see her."

He was gone before I could respond to this, melting into the darkness.

The clock struck five.

"I have to go," I told Far, putting blankets about her--a useless gesture, for myself more than for her. She stared at me, and my eyes slid away from her accusatory gaze.

"You go to steal another soul," she said, voice flat. It would do no good to lie, so I didn't, didn't say anything, just filled another bowl with rice from the pot and set it on the table beside her.

I turned to leave. "Please eat something," I whispered again, my parting words, because I knew it wouldn't matter if I asked her to stay. She would do what she wanted, as she always had. She would leave the shack if she wanted, would die again if she wanted, and there was nothing I could do this time to stop her. To save her.

"You had no right," she said, and the words latched onto my heart like leeches, slithered out the door with me, into the darkness.

Her mouth was warm and soft--softer than anything, everything in the city--and it held mine captive. Between kisses, I gasped for breath. Her fingers tightly wrapped my own, and then they were around my waist, pulling me close, closer, a shift of skin and velvet that made my eyes roll back as her lips moved down my neck, as her sweet breath blew across my skin, her hair draped upon me like a swathe of darkness. I felt...everything.

"I love you," I whispered to her, put my hands in her hair, arched against her. "I love you," I said again, when she did not respond.

Her mouth devoured me; her tongue and fingers claimed me as her own.

But she remained, even in the most sublime of those moments, utterly silent.

I knew her on sight, as Tryx had promised. She wept in a corner booth, black death-veil shrouding her face but not concealing the shudder of her shoulders, not muffling the discordant sound of her sobs. I made my way to the back, sat in the booth beside her and stared straight ahead.

"I'm your Runner," I said, voice soft; she inclined her head toward me. "Who are you looking for?"

Her fingers grazed a picture on the tabletop--a man with reddish curls, haunted eyes, full lips.

"Please," she said, and pressed coins into my

hand.

I closed my eyes, saw the man's face hovering there, embedded and suspended. I was too tired to do this, but the weight of the precious metal in my hand felt familiar, good and right. It had been too long since I'd Run for real, for coin. I could do it; I was the best, and this woman needed me. She rubbed at her face beneath her veil, and I stood, nodded.

"Stay here until I return. Or, if eight chimes come and I'm not back, find someone else," I said, clearing my throat.

"Find someone else?" Her voice caught on the last word. "But there is no one else!"

I shrugged and left, skin chilled. It had never been like this before. There were always Runners, always Robbers. I shook my head, shuddered, tried not to think about the implications; still, a half dozen terrible fears crawled up my spine and took root in bone.

I made the chalk circle in an abandoned warehouse, listening to the click and clack of stone paws overhead as the gargoyles made ready for their nightly rounds. "Please keep me safe, for her, for Far," I beseeched everyone and nothing as I stepped both boots into the chalked circle, felt the darkness rise up and seize me.

The stone lions looked down in disgust.

The Prehend floated between them.

I opened my mouth to scream, but there was no time; it was too late. She drifted forward, fast as lightning, fast as heartache, jaw unhinged to gobble me up.

Blackness.

"Who is she?" I whispered to Tryx, biting my lip and shifting from foot to foot. He looked me over,

scowled, and shook his head.

"She calls herself Far."

The woman walked through the dark markets, head bowed to each person she encountered, watching their hands whenever they gestured. She wore a dazed expression at first, but--gradually--that fell from her face like a discarded mask. She said little--listening, instead, smiling occasionally. That's what made her stand out. Few people in the city smiled. She was different.

"When did she arrive?"

"How would I know that?" He shrugged. "Go talk to her."

"She's new," I said, more to myself than to him. "She looks happy."

"Give her a day or two more. She'll change," he said.

I watched her, and I gathered wisps of courage to craft a heart. Then I walked up to her and waved my fingers in front of her face. "Hello. My name is Mana. Do you...need anything?"

She smiled at me, and I felt myself smiling back.

"Hello, Mana. I am Far," she said. "Do you know how to get out of the city?"

My mouth slackened, and I shook my head. "You don't...get out... How long have you been here?"

She looked up at me shyly, dark eyes shining. "I don't know. This is all so strange. Isn't it? I feel as if I'm in a dream..."

"I've been here for a long time. I can help you. Let me help you." I offered her my hand.

She smiled again. All that I was before, desired before, disappeared, replaced by only her.

I could not live without Far.

Two

They didn't name the city. They had no need to name the city. No one ever asked what it was called, why it *was*, why we were here. They accepted it all, complacent, and they ate and they fucked and they chatted with each other on the grimy streets, and they avoided the Gray Coats and the gargoyles, and they lived to die.

No one ever asked why.

I did.

Mana always told me that I'd be found out, that they'd come for me because I asked questions. I couldn't understand why she thought that, where the knowledge--or the notion--came from. The Gray Coats were menacing in appearance, but I had never seen them exert force against anyone. People weren't ever taken away, didn't disappear; they just died.

And, oh, how I wanted to die, had always wanted to die, for as long as I could remember.

"Be quiet, Far," Mana would tell me, feeding me taffy as if I were stupid, as if I could be distracted. She didn't mean to condescend--I knew she didn't--but it made me bristle when she kissed me so I'd shut up, when she fucked me so I'd still my tongue. She told me, over and over, how much she loved me, but I'd wipe at my mouth with the back of my hand, wipe off her kisses, and I would get *so angry*.

"Why don't you wonder why we're here?" I asked, trying to hold her at arm's length, trying to get her to stop her advances. "Why don't you wonder about anything?"

"All I care about is you," she'd say, and she'd kiss me, and when she kissed me, I knew what she said was true.

I loved her. I did. I loved her so much, despite how fucked up everything was, as we were, as the city was. I loved her with all that I had, all I had left, tried to show her the best I could when we lay together, when it became something beautiful. But I was too afraid to say it, to tell her. I was too afraid to acknowledge something lovely in this ugly place.

And now look where we are.
I regret that. Fuck, I regret everything.

"That's impossible," I told Tryx, trying to hold my voice steady, digging my dead nails into my palms. His face was empty, neutral, but when he bowed his head, I saw the mask crack. He dealt with death and grieving every day, and he marshaled the Runners--when there still *were* Runners--but even he seemed surprised that Mana was gone.

"She didn't come back from After." He folded his arms, eyes lowered. "So--it's over."

I didn't believe it. Couldn't. "No," I said, like a child. "She's the best. She's the best Runner in the city. Didn't she say that every day? Wasn't it always true?"

"Hey. At least someone loved you enough to do this for you." When he said "this," he gestured at my body, the body I felt rotting from the inside out. "She brought you back because she gave a shit. I mean--did you even understand how much she loved you?"

I stared at him, anger coursing through me like my blood used to.

"Yes, I understood," I told him, and I left, shuffled out of the warehouse, comically slow on my dead-weight legs.

"You didn't act like you did," he called to my back.

His words hit me like a blow.

I was angry, I wanted to scream at him. I was angry, and I had a right to be angry. But it didn't mean that I didn't love her...

I collapsed in an alleyway, enjoying a grim satisfaction as the earth smacked against my body—no, not my body anymore. A cadaver's body. I didn't feel the impact. I felt nothing. I put my head in my hands, tried to think.

I was always *different*. I didn't belong here, knew that from the moment I had sentience. I despised how complacent the people were, hated the system they obeyed so blindly. Waiting to die? What sort of fucked up existence was that?

I was an aberration, an outsider; I didn't belong. But Mana thought I did--or at least that I belonged with her. It made me sick, the guilt from wanting to leave, wanting to *die*. She would look at me, her brown eyes filled with tears, and she would press me close, as if the solidity of her body could erase my need to escape.

Sometimes it did. Sometimes it was enough. But then she would have to Run, and I remembered all over again why I hated this city...

I pressed my head against my knees, tried to make myself smaller, as small as I felt.

Now I was a Reanima, and there was no way out.

And Mana was gone.

I don't know what to do.

Anger burned inside of me, boiled through me, hot, almost painful. It felt red and deep as muscle.

The Reanima couldn't truly weep; they had no tears to let fall. But I did my best; I cried out, a deep, guttural cry, ferocious, as I fell over, as I beat my hands against the pavement, pleased by the hard, fleshy*smack*. I was trapped in a place I despised without the person who was my only reason for staying, for living...

You didn't act like you did.

I stared at the stone wall in front of me and hated Tryx with all of my heart.

I *loved* her. Didn't she know I loved her?

Didn't I ever tell her?

I couldn't remember telling her.

I wanted to die. I wanted to die now, as an undead *thing*, more than I had ever wanted it when I was alive. I wanted blackness, oblivion; I wanted an end to my torment, to my anger, my hatred, to my patheticness.

Surely there must be some way to speed up this slow death that was my reanimated life. That no one knew of any way meant nothing. No one had ever wanted it, needed it as much as I did.

I laid there, hands balled into fists, stiff and fuming, and tried to plot my second death.

There was the scrabbling of claws on stone, and I lifted my eyes up and up and up the overhead building's side, saw a gargoyle walking down the wall, vertically. I sat, watched it.

Perhaps the gargoyles have come to take me away, after all.

Mana was always afraid of the gargoyles, but I almost liked them. Great stone beasts, none of them alike, with fearsome faces, distended jaws that swiveled, eyes that glinted of quartz in the darkness. They looked like nightmares, but they'd never done any harm to me.

The gargoyle saw me staring, must have seen me staring, for it began to click and clack down the wall in my direction.

It settled onto the earth beside me, crouching, pointed ears flicking back and forth, making snappy, pebbly sounds. Its sparking eyes turned on me.

"Hello," I said, my voice hollow but steady, unafraid.

The gargoyle opened its mouth and returned, low

and grumbly, "Hello."

We watched one another for a long, still moment.

The clock chimed twelve.

I stood, rigid, scarcely able to bend my decaying legs and spine for the necessary movements. The gargoyle didn't stir when I tottered off to the left, resting my hand against the wall. But it continued to watch me.

"Are you Far?" asked the gargoyle then, startling me.

"Yes," I replied. And I thought, *She was right.* Mana was right. The Gray Coats and the gargoyles searched the city for treasonous inhabitants, and somehow, some way, they had found out my thoughts, had heard me speak, knew what I had done and why I had done it, and they were going to drag me away now, to some dank, dark prison--though not much danker or darker than the city itself (how could it be?)--and I would rot there forever because I dared to ask questions.

Well. If that's the way it has to be.

The gargoyle stared at me, and I wondered for a moment whether its expression was one of bemusement. Its grotesque mouth cracked up at the corners, as if it might be smiling.

It sidled closer, dragging its distended stone belly over the earth.

"I know the way out. You want out, don't you?"

I gaped. "Out?"

"Out of the city."

Out.

"How do you know that?" I hissed, crouching low beside its great head, which the gargoyle shook left to right, swinging the stone hoop earring in its big stone ear.

"I just know," it growled at me, peering up, looking imperious. It repeated: "You want out, don't you?"

A strange seizing locked up my insides, and for a

25

moment, I couldn't speak. My eyes narrowed; my mind raced. I fell fully to the ground and let my tongue lead my thoughts.

"If you know that much, then do you know where Mana is?"

"Not nearby," and it chuckled, as if to itself. It didn't stop laughing when it saw my sickened expression-- in fact, it laughed harder. I dug my nails into my thighs to quell my anger.

"Don't get so worked up," the gargoyle sighed, pressing its jaw to the ground and stretching. "I know where your girl is."

Your girl.

My girl.

I rose to my knees beside the gargoyle, but one of my limbs faltered, and I reached out, caught myself on the creature's great head. It looked hard at me but offered no protest, let me push off so that I sat hunched over in a squat in the filthy alley, monster and monster, together.

"I...I need to find Mana," I said, because they were the only words that mattered to me now.

The gargoyle claimed to know the way out. *Out.* That was all I had ever wanted.

Before I lost Mana.

"Will you help me?" I asked. It seemed right, to ask.

"My name is Lock," said the gargoyle, stretching its thick neck out further.

I didn't even think about it--my arm extended, and my hand scratched behind the gargoyle's ear. It growled, and I started back before I realized that the growl was actually a purr.

"I will help you," it said.

I had no reason to trust it.

But I did.

"You can only find Mana if you get out, and you can only get out one way," said the gargoyle, clicking along the outer wall of the building with me sprawled across its back. I felt ludicrous but strangely secure.

"How do you know the way out?"

"Do you ever stop asking questions?"

I smiled a little. Mana used to ask me that.

"No."

It growled in response. Then it said, "Get off."

I did.

The gargoyle curled through a broken window, stone scraping against jagged glass. I peered inside the building. There, on the floor of the warehouse, was one of Mana's chalk Runner circles. I recognized the lines and curves of it, the language of the dead, and recoiled. It was because of this, because of Running, that she was gone.

"Be brave," said Lock, shifting its body into a seated position on a wide ledge beneath the window. One big, four-clawed stone hand gestured at me, and I crept through the window--careful of the glass even though it could no longer hurt the likes of me--and sat beside Lock. The tips of my toes grazed against a tabletop set against the wall.

"The only way out is through that." Lock pointed at the chalk circle. "We must go to After. We cannot get to After without the circle. And no gargoyle may operate the circle." Two sparking eyes caught my gaze, held me fast. "Only a human may do so."

"Human?" I scoffed. "I'm not human anymore."

"You're human enough," the gargoyle growled. "Go." It urged me with a powerful clamp of claws on my shoulder. "Try."

I didn't know what to do. I'd never watched Mana cast the circle, had never seen her use one. She'd told me what it was like to fade into After once or twice, but that was long ago, or perhaps not so long, but my brain was already rotting.

I placed a hand upon Lock's great head—the creature bent it toward me, offering its support--slid down to the table, steadied myself, and lowered my body to the floor without a scrap of dignity. Lock joined me, pressed close against me, and together we stepped across the circle.

It was too easy.

There was blackness, and then soft light.

Next to these two stone lions, Lock was a toy, tiny, unimpressive. The lions towered over both of us, their eyes flashing like the gargoyle's.

"What is the meaning of this?" said the lion on the left, opening and closing its wide stone jaws. "Who are you? Why are you here?"

I ignored the questions and looked beyond. Between the lions, there was a massive cave opening, like a too-large, eager mouth. Mana had described this scene to me enough times; it was the entrance to After. And the stone lions guarded the entrance.

I stared up at the pair of them. Mana had told me they were simple.

"Hello," I began. They stared at me, unamused. I cleared my throat, tried again: "Hello. I've come from the city."

"They all come from the city, trying to take back what is not theirs," said the lion on the right. "Give us one reason not to eat you up."

Eat me up? I bristled.

"What right do you have?" I asked brazenly. Lock's stone shoulder beneath my hand seemed to soften somehow, and shake. The gargoyle was either laughing or trembling. Perhaps a little of both.

The lions didn't respond right away. I wondered,

in the lull, whether anyone had asked them such a question before. They seemed, quite honestly, stumped.

"I need to go into After," I said, realizing only after I'd spoken the words that I didn't know *why* I must enter After, hadn't asked Lock why yet, and my rashness brought on new anger, this time at myself. What was I getting myself into? Was Mana here? Had the gargoyle led me astray?

The two lions glanced at one another.

"We guard After from people like you," said the lion on the left, but it didn't sound half so confident as before.

"After is filled with beings exactly like me. Why keep me out? What exactly are you guarding?"

Silence again. Lock nudged me, nodded encouragement.

"We're guarding souls..." said the lion on the right, looking to his companion. "Isn't that what we're guarding?"

"I thought we were guarding the Recycler Chamber. It's not as if we were given a list of tasks," said the lion on the left.

"No, there's only one task. To guard After."

"But from what? And for what?"

"We're not supposed to question our dictated objectives-- "

"Did we have any of those to start with? And who dictated them?"

"Well, we must--I suppose-- How should I know any more than you do?"

Lock and I slipped unnoticed between the bickering lions, and a thrill raced through me, chased by a shiver, when we entered the gaping maw into After.

After... This is After.

We were in.

"They really are stupid, just like Mana said," I

whispered to Lock, who flicked pointy ears at me, shook its head.

"Questions change things," the gargoyle said.

"No," I whispered back. "Answers do."

A line of glowing, billowing white pillars drifted before us. Each pillar had a face. I recognized one, then another. It was a line of souls, winding toward a distant hill, atop of which shone a white chamber.

"What are we doing here, Lock?" I asked the gargoyle, my hand braced on its sturdy shoulder.

"Waiting," it said, glancing back to the cave opening, and then staring again at the beginning of the line, as if it watched for something.

"Waiting for what?"

"The Prehend."

No.

My memories were rotting, but I would never forget the stories Mana had told me of the monster who haunts After, the Prehend. Could never forget the terror in Mana's eyes when she spoke of her.

I stepped away from the gargoyle, shook my head.

"That's your-- The Prehend? Lock. Why? What happens when we see her? What do we have to--"

"We need her to devour us."

Everything fell away. I fell away, down to the ground, and my head smacked stone hard. I hadn't fainted; Reanima couldn't faint. I'd simply stopped concentrating on standing up. I shifted awkwardly, propped myself up on an elbow.

"That's your plan? That's how we get out?" I swatted in the gargoyle's direction, but it evaded me, stared at me. Sighed.

"What did you think? That we would find a door, walk through? The only way out of the City is to be eaten up by the Prehend."

"You didn't say-- "

"You didn't ask."

Anger began to lick along the edges of my thoughts.

"How do you know that this will work? How do you know that we'll get out, that we won't just cease to be? Lock, how do I know this isn't a gargoyle's trick?"

Lock gazed into my eyes with its own huge, sparking ones. There was nothing of trickery within them, only of sadness, of great weight, of an unending life.

"Mana is beyond the Prehend. If you want to see her again, you must be devoured."

There was a soft sound, a sibilant shushing, and--ahead, in the line—I saw a billowing of white cloth, of glowing flesh, of mouth open, teeth flashing in the half-light of After. She had eyes, but they were black, far blacker than my own, and she was smiling as she floated beside the line of souls, staring down at them as a beast might regard a night's meal.

"You wanted answers," said Lock then, as I pressed my shoulder blades against the earth, felt its solidity beneath me. "You can have them. You were brave enough to ask the questions. What will you dare for the truth?"

The Prehend drifted farther down the line, nearer to us. Miraculously, terrifyingly, somehow…she had not seen us yet.

The cave opening was at our backs. I could still turn around. I could still run. I could still leave.

Lock laid down beside me, turned its head toward the vile apparition, and waited.

"Fuck," I muttered, and I climbed onto the gargoyle's back.

When the Prehend lifted her black gaze and saw us at last, a sound came out of her mouth, a sound that tore me up, that sliced through me like a blade; it was a scream so terrible, I felt I might die from the echo of it. If I weren't already dead.

I closed my eyes, gripped Lock's ears, and surrendered to the absolute dark of her descent.

Wind.
Screaming.
Wind.
Falling.
Wind...
...Impact.

Three

"Fuck," I whispered, just to make certain I *could* still whisper, could still use my voice, was actually still *existent*, that this was not oblivion, that I was--for all intents and purposes--all right.

Everything ached.

Which was odd. I was a Reanima. Reanima felt nothing.

I felt...*everything*.

I opened my eyes.

Light. Light everywhere, strange orange light that filtered through the dust and fog and debris in the air, touching my face like hands, like a physical thing. I looked up, and there was an orb above me, filled with— no, made of light.

I...I know what it is. It's a sun. The sun. I know what the sun is.

How had I ever forgotten it?

I tried to stand, slumped back into the dirt. There

were odd pieces of trash around me, wood, metal--all twisted and crumpled or melded together. I couldn't see beyond the length of my body; everything was wreathed in a hazy blur. I couldn't breathe, kept coughing, put my hand up, touched my nose and realized that I was actually breathing. Breathing! I never thought I'd breathe again. I looked down at my fingers, saw that my nails were pink, that my skin was dirty but *not rotting*.

How...can this be? What's happening? Where am I?

A shift beside me, earth moving, and Lock's head appeared up and out of the dirt, spitting earth from his great mouth. (I had decided that Lock was a he.)

"Are you all right?" he asked, and I was startled by the change of his voice. Before, it was gravely, deep...but now it was ten voices smashed into one, like ten people talking at once. I stared at him, slid backwards as he struggled up and out of the ground, shook himself, and looked down on me, eyes still sparking, stone eyebrows raised, bemused.

"What's the matter, Far?"

Again, that collision of voices. I stood, found that I was able to now, and I brushed off my hands on my filthy pants.

I sighed, breathed out.

"What's the matter?" I repeated, and my voice sounded normal, though a little dull. I didn't have ten voices. "Where are we? What's happening? Why am I no longer a Reanima?"

"Don't tell me you're disappointed." He stretched, lengthening his back, arching.

I covered my mouth, wide-eyed.

"I'm not...undead anymore?"

The gargoyle shook his massive head. "No, you are not."

I ran my hands over my arms, my breasts, my

33

stomach, my hips. It all felt solid, and when I paused, I felt the blood rushing, thrumming through me, warm and liquid. I was alive.

I coughed again, cherished the air moving in my lungs even as the taste of it burned my tongue.

"Where are we?" I asked, looking up at the sun. Gray clouds, the size and shape of missiles, scuttled across its yellow path.

Missiles.

I knew that word.

Lock padded up beside me, and I rested a hand upon his hulking shoulder.

"Come with me," he said, ten quiet voices urging me onward.

Together, we walked into the smoke, the mist, the blur of this new world.

The trees were gnarled and clawing up at the clouded sky, their bark embedded with shrapnel and broken bits of metal, shining in the light of the covered sun. Their towering shapes materialized out of the gloom, crouched over us like clawed monsters. I flinched again and again, leaning heavily against Lock's bulk.

We began a downward descent, and my heart was filled with questions, but I kept coughing, couldn't draw in a single ragged breath that didn't burn my throat, so I swallowed my words and saved my voice.

We were in a bowl of the earth, enclosed by walls of rock-studded dirt on all sides. When my eyes stopped tearing, when I stumbled for the thousandth time, caught my breath, and could see again--slightly--I noticed it: a human-shaped shadow close enough that, if I moved forward only a few paces, I might reach out and touch it. I didn't want to touch it. I recoiled from it until Lock stepped forward, pulling me behind him, and I fought him, stumbled again--once, twice--and then I *was* close enough to touch, to clearly see…her.

34

Mana.

She stood, eyes wide and open, staring at me. Her arms were down at her sides, and her clothes were just as tattered as before, as always, but she didn't look hurt. She looked alive.

I didn't know what to do in that moment. Emotion gripped me, and I tripped one final step and embraced her, and I felt a wave of shame wash over me, but--*fuck it all, I'm crying*--I held her close, held her unyielding form so close. I'd found her. I was swallowed by a monster, and I *found* her.

She didn't move, didn't reciprocate, didn't touch me.

"Mana," I whispered, leaning back, peering at her unmoving face. A chill passed through me. Her eyes stared ahead, her mouth drawn in a straight, still line.

I stepped backward, holding myself, feeling a tremor of fear move through me.

Lock was not there. He was gone.

"Far," said Mana, a single whispered word, and it was Lock's voice, Mana's voice, *every* voice, all voices and no voice, all at once. I opened my mouth and shut it, holding out my hand.

"Mana?" I said, the syllables uncertain.

She didn't move for the longest moment, stood there still as a gargoyle at noon, but then she exhaled and shook her head. Her eyes focused, she rubbed her face, and she saw me, truly saw me, and she stepped forward, *dashed* forward, with that wide, sweet grin on her face. She picked me up and twirled me around, and I was in her arms, and she peppered my face, my shoulders, my hands with kisses.

"Far," she whispered again, and before anything changed, before everything could fall apart into tiny mirrored pieces, I took her face in both of my hands, stared into her eyes and said it.

"I love you." My voice was small. "I'm so sorry I never said it. I do--I love you."

She worked her mouth, her eyebrows, but she leaned forward and kissed me and said nothing--and at the same time, everything--and only when she'd pulled away, smiled at me, caressed my face, she returned in that eerie ten-voice, "I love you, too, Far."

She was crying.

I held her close, so close, my head pressed against her chest.

And that was when it began to shatter.

I couldn't hear her heartbeat.

No.

I didn't want to come out of this; I didn't want it to end, this moment in which everything was still fine, when I wasn't *questioning,* wasn't thinking about where we were and when we were and *how* we were.

But the moment was lost. I backed away, hands on the curves of Mana's hips, and I looked up into her beloved brown eyes and didn't know what to say to her, other than this: "Mana, what's going on?"

And she sighed, and her shoulders slumped, and I knew--as I'd known from the beginning--that it was *all* wrong.

"How do you feel?" she asked in that everything/nothing voice. I closed my mouth, moved away.

"Mana, answer the question."

She spread her hands, turned her eyes from me. For a long moment, she remained silent. But then she said, "Would you destroy all of this…" She took my hand, held it between her own. "…for the truth?"

"The truth doesn't destroy-- "

She shook her head at me. "It does, here and now. It does in this, Far."

I swallowed, coughed, sat down, placing my head

in my hands.

"Why do I feel that I've not really found you?" I asked, and then I was crying. I hated that I was crying, would have done anything not to cry. I loved her. I'd *found* her. But I felt like I'd lost her all over again.

Was this Mana? I didn't think she was Mana, not really. And if she was not Mana, then I had never really told her that I loved her. Then she still didn't know.

I looked up at the woman staring down at me.

If she wasn't Mana…then who was she?

She crouched beside me, touched my shoulder gently.

"You came looking for me."

I shrugged her off, put my head in my hands again. "I came looking for Mana. You're not Mana."

She sighed, sat down at my side. "Yes, I am."

Hope bubbled unbidden in my heart, but her expression hadn't changed. It contained no joy, merely remorse and sadness and pity—for me or for her, I could not tell.

"Please," I said, "tell me what's happening."

She closed her mouth, looked past me into the swirling gloom. "Everything…everything that has been done has been done for you, Far. Though you may not see that, or understand it, now, I hope you will--in time."

I   blinked   at   her, waited.

"I am Mana," she said, turning to face me, her eyes bright and flashing. "But I am also Lock. And I am Tryx and the Prehend and…" She bowed her head. "I am After. I am the whole city. And…I am none of those things."

She picked up a handful of earth. "I am this, if I am wholly truthful. I am, at my deepest core, this wasteland."

I stared, eyes wide, uncomprehending. My mouth moved, and my heart tumbled, and--laughably--the first thing I could think to say was, "You...knew this all along? Mana-- *As* Mana, you knew what you were, and you toyed with me?"

She shook her head, almost imperceptibly. "My constructs, *this* construct--" She pressed her hand against her stomach. "It had free will, had no part of my sentience, until it left the City as a result of its own choices."

I watched her, distrustful, confused. "I don't understand."

"You remember nothing of before," she said sadly. "Let me show you." And then she lifted up her hands, and--gentle, soft--she cradled my face with her fingers.

There was a flash, far brighter than the mist-robed sun.

Bodies.

Everywhere bodies, swollen, bloating. Earth, no grass, trees broken, stumbling, stumbling, can't breathe, can't see, can't breathe. Where is everyone? Everyone can't be dead. I scream until my throat is hoarse, until the earth begins to soften, turn to sand, until I crumple at the base of something tall and metal, and I wait, like everyone else, to die.

Arms--lifting me, gentle, holding me, carrying me into darkness, and I can breathe again, and I am so tired, and I sleep.

I opened my eyes.

Mana's expression was a mystery to me, and she looked away when my eyes filled with tears.

"The end..." I whispered. "The world...the bombs... I couldn't find anyone alive. I *remember*."

"That I know of, to my farthest reaches, you are one of the only survivors," she said, and she held up her hands when I began to weep. "But I do not reach forever.

There could be others."

I pressed my hands to my face, rocked back and forth. I had forgotten.

"You," I whispered. "You made me forget."

"I took you in, and I gave you safety. Life. I...had built a construct." She ran her finger along the skin of her arm. "I built the city. I had memories and dreams and nightmares, collected from the people who once lived here. Seeped into my soil. I was alive, knew I was alive, and I needed to make some sense of that. So I built the construct to help me understand life, and to keep it, hold its memory..." She spread her hands. "I did not expect a real human to find it, but, once she had, I knew the greater purpose for its existence."

I breathed out, coughed again, hard this time, unable to breathe for a long moment. My eyes streamed until I couldn't see.

Mana rested her fingers against my neck...and I calmed, took in a ragged gulp of air.

"Are you God?" I whispered, because it was the only thought my mind could gather.

"No, Far," she said, and she smiled a little. "I am only a wasteland. But I am capable of love."

"You were the earth?"

"Yes, if that helps you understand. I am a piece of the earth, a part of it. I don't know why I feel, or why I understand, or why I can create. I believe that there are more of me--whatever I am--upon this world, crafting constructs just as I have. Through you, Far, I have not felt alone."

"How can a place feel alone?" I asked her. My heart beat steadier now, and I picked up her hand, turned it over. It felt soft and warm...real. It felt like Mana.

"I have loved you, Far," she whispered, leaning closer to me.

I didn't know what to do, how to feel. When she

kissed me, so soft, so imploring, I melted, broke apart. It was Mana--it had always been Mana.

I wrapped my arms about her neck, and I kissed her in return.

"But..." I leaned back, so that our foreheads touched. "Why? Why the Gray Coats and the Prehend? Why After?"

"It evolved," she said, tracing a fingernail over my collarbone. "The memories, the dreams, the nightmares--they were alive, in small, perfect ways. Like humanity, the world evolved. And I think, somehow, it was preparing itself for this change--for your evolution. "

I thought of the Prehend, the Runners lost to her devouring. The City had been changing long before my death, and before Mana's.

I pulled Mana close to me, marveling, trying my best to accept, to not question.

"You and I can create it new now, however you wish," she whispered. "We will create a home together. A sanctuary, a safe place, locked away and safe--forever."

"It was all an illusion?"

The sun began to set, and the darkness began to grow.

"If someone believes in an illusion hard enough, for long enough, it can become the strongest thing, the realest and truest thing."

"Am I...dead?"

She drew back from me and paled a little, but she shook her head. "Not...yet."

I swallowed, coughed. "Are you keeping me alive?"

"In a way."

"You love me?"

"Always."

She was holding my hand gently, as if it might break apart, dissolve to dust. I had so many questions, and

I knew that--eventually--she would give me all of the answers, and when I opened my mouth, her eyebrows lifted, and she laughed, and she spoke with ten voices, a thousand voices, one voice--Mana's voice.

"Recreate the world with me, Far," she said, and kissed me, a wasteland, a woman, a future.

So we did.

THE WITCH SEA

I knew what she was. When she came up the path, feet quiet, deliberate, I knew it from the way she moved, the webbing between her bare toes, how she faltered when she reached the lighthouse landing, like she had never seen things like stairs before. I knew, and I said nothing, because we were all, in our own way, monsters.

"Nor," she said, sticking out her hand as if she expected me to shake it.

"That's what he named you?" I asked, arms folded before me.

"Yes," she said.

I did not touch her.

She had come by boat. She had to. They could not touch the saltwater. He wouldn't let them, and they obeyed him.

If they touched the water, if they slipped or tripped or dared, the spray made them scream, mouths wide, tongues distended. A wave made them crumple, skin sagging and bloated, until their flesh fell apart, obliterated by the blue, leaving a clean, new creature beneath: sometimes a seal, wet coat slick, brown eyes still human. Sometimes a walrus, growing until the human body burst apart, revealing tusk and tooth. Sometimes it was a small, silver fish that flopped helplessly until it reached the water—or did not, lying, rotting, in the sunshine.

She wasn't human, Nor. But neither was I.

"They call you a witch," she said, smiling, moving facial muscles into toothy grin, like a silent growl. "Are the stories true? Do you keep the fish from the bay so that the people starve? Do you dance in the moonlight? Did you sell your soul?"

"I am not what you think I am," I said, and let her into my house, with her wet brown eyes and hands she kept clasped in front of her. If I had shut the door, if I had kept her out, she would have remained on my island, anyway. He had sent her. We both knew he had sent her. And he was dauntless.

"They call you Meriel," she said then, sitting down at the table stiffly. "Is that your name?"

"It is."

"You hate us."

"I do not."

"You hate me?"

A seal's eyes are innocent, contain no malice, no human anger or rage, and though she showed a human shape now, she was still seal. Her eyes were limpid, round, deep when she looked up at me, hands on the table, widespread. They were webbed, too, her fingers, but only a little. He was getting better.

"I do not hate you," I told her. It was not a lie.

"He hopes that you will reconsider his offer, you know. He is not a bad man. He never was a bad man."

"No," I said, and it was so tired.

"I will come again tomorrow," she said, and she stood, too sudden, jerky. "I hope that you will reconsider, too, Meriel." Her voice was warm and soft, skin smooth, brown, beautiful.

She held out her hand again as she departed. I did not take it.

I watched her as she walked away and down the

dirt path. Her hips swung gently from side to side, the thin skirt lying along her curves.

He had tried everything else, and this was a last resort; I knew that. Again, he would fail. She would fail.

But I thought of her that night, hand over my own breast, listening to the crash of the waves against the rock outside my window, watching the faint flash of silver upon the ceiling, reflection of my finely woven net of spells that kept the fish out of the bay.

In the morning, I checked the line, standing on the shore, hands extended, feeling the push and pull of the tide and waves as I crawled over every inch of the silver net with my head and heart, testing it and pulling it and mending it where mends were needed, shaping the magic in long strands, crisscrossed—always crisscrossed.

The bright sunshine reflected off of the water, blinding me, and I did not see her approach in the little boat, did not see her get out and climb the path to me. I squinted, blinked, and suddenly, she was there, as if by magic. I rose from my work, and I went to meet her, bright spots along my vision outlining her in a riot of color.

"Good morning, Meriel," she said, and she curtsied. Her movements were more certain than the day before, nearly graceful. It did not take some of them long to get used to the land, to how their new limbs and muscles worked. She seemed almost human now.

"Good morning, Nor," I told her.

"He wishes me to ask you to change your mind, Meriel. He has said that he will double his offer, if only you will cease."

"I will not," I said, and it was laughable, the formalities: how prettily he'd dressed her up this morning; the doubling or tripling of his offer of gold, of house and land and a hundred thousand things he hoped might tempt me. They did not. They would not. I wondered when he would tire of this.

The sea was patient. He was patient. But patience could wear thin.

"Oh," was what she said, and it was obvious that she was disappointed, confused, that she had thought today would be the day when I would smile, nod, give in to his demands. She opened her mouth and shut it, so like a fish. Beneath it all, they were always like fish.

"Go back," I said, not unkindly. "Tell him 'never.'"

"He will not accept that, you know." She lowered her chin, looked over her shoulder, stepped closer. She smelled of salt. "He will send me back every day, Meriel."

"As you will," I said.

She left.

I was born on Bound Island. My mother pushed me out, and--that same night--had to tend to the nets. Back then, it was roughly every seven days that breaks would occur, that the magic would have to be woven back into the silver strands. Now it was every day.

Nothing living could slip through the nets and enter the bay. Not intact. If it slipped through, it would...change. And it would become his--Galo's.

So I tended the nets.

Once, twice, a million times, I asked my mother to tell me the story of Galo. I remember her familiar movements as she banked the fire, drew me close, traced a protective circle in the dirt about our forms.

She always whispered it.

Long ago, before man or woman or stories, there was the sea. It crashed and roared and boiled, churning life into being. At the center of the sea swam Galo. He was larger than the island, larger than the bay, with four limbs that turned into tentacles that turned into hoofed legs, and a long, equine nose with teeth as long as oars and sharp as stars. He had been in the sea from the beginning, rising from the muck and mud at the bottom of the world, fully formed. He was the oldest sea god and the most powerful. Storms came from him; whirlpools followed his finned hooves. His heart was black, and he knew only chaos, and everything in the sea feared him mightily.

Land came then. And some things from the sea ventured upon it, exchanging their fins for legs, their gills for lungs. Man came into the world, and the sea was forsaken. The men forgot their origins, forgot their fathers who had crept from the salt, and they shook their fists at the water. They built boats and crossed the seas and believed they had conquered the waves.

Forgotten, too, Galo slept at the bottom of the world. One day, he awoke and saw how much had changed, saw how man defiled his mother, the sea, saw how there was no reverence in man's heart for the ocean that had given him life. Galo's own black heart grew even blacker, and he thought and he thought, and he formed a plan.

He changed from his equine form, shed his fins and his sharp teeth, and he crawled upon the land, now a man. He shaped a town from mud, and he turned back to the waters and lifted his new arms. Out of the ocean crept all manner of creatures: the whales and the fish and the octopus and the shark, and they shed their animal forms and become people, too.

"We will make a great army," Galo said to them, "and we will punish the humans for their sacrilege. We will destroy them on land, we will devour them upon the sea, and man will cease to be. The ocean will reign again."

The sea people, as one, gave a great shout and

said, "We will obey you, Galo, for you are mighty and strong." And more creatures began to emerge from the sea, and more and more, until the beach teemed with people who had shark eyes and whale hearts, dripping hair and tusks for teeth.

But then the march of animals stopped abruptly. For, at the mouth of the bay, upon our own Bound Island-- though it was not known as such back then--stepped a witch. Your grandmother, Meriel, for whom you are named. She drew down a star, and from its shimmering bulk, she fashioned something so large, so ludicrous, it stretched across the entire mouth of the bay, both ways.

She said, "While those of my bloodline live, Galo, you will never get your creatures. I curse you to remain in the town you have built, trapped and unable to summon the sea to your aid."

And, because he was small, a man, and no longer mighty, the curse stuck to Galo like a barnacle.

I sometimes wondered at the audacity of Grandmother. The oldest god of the sea took the form of a mortal man, and she wove a net and curse so tightly that he was spellbound by it. Did she ever fear retribution? Did she ever look through the curtains of the tiny cottage at night and watch the people come to the edge of the water, all along the beach of the bay? Did she watch them stand, silent, looking out to the sea they could no longer touch, would never touch again, as long as the curse remained? Galo was cruel. While he must remain in the town he had fashioned, he demanded that all of his creations did, too.

The people stood beneath the stars along the shore and looked out to the sea, mourning its loss. And they cursed my grandmother.

And my mother.

And now me.

I used to think this was bigger than all of us. My mother told me the story of Galo and of my grandmother and how we must remain, for all time, upon the island. We were the axis of the world, she said, as she dusted my nose with flour or tossed me into the air. We were important.

My mother told me, too, of how she'd seduced my father to the island. How I would also have to seduce a man in order to keep our bloodline alive. If our bloodline died out, the curse would break. And the world would end.

She'd said it all so matter-of-factly, hands upon the washboard, drawing the tea towels over the ridges again and again, scrubbing the stains out. I watched her hands go up and down, and I felt a remorse like fire rake through my stomach, my heart. I would not seduce a man, and there was no simple way to tell my mother this truth. So I never did.

But I was so lonely.

My mother had left me the island, a legacy, and a stone. The first two were burdens; the last was my saving grace in those hard days following her death. It was a plain stone, the size of my palm, and clear. When I stared within it, it showed me what I wished to see. Not fantasies but facts, as they happened--real, true life.

I watched the townsfolk and Galo in the stone's depths. If they ever suspected an outsider saw them, observed them, they made no gestures to indicate it. They moved within the stone like little pictures, stories, lives I could see but never touch.

Sometimes, when I was little, I stole away my mother's stone, and I peered into it and asked it for friends. It showed me the inhabitants of the bay town, then, too, showed me the women with hair like tentacles, the men with shark eyes and sharp teeth, and I wondered why it presented me with visions so contrary to my request.

But over time, over the years, I understood. The sea people did become my friends. In a way. They were all I knew.

When Nor left me for the second time, I dusted my hands against my apron pockets and climbed up and into the lighthouse. The shack along the lighthouse proper, where a lighthouse tender should have lived, had long since disintegrated, crumbling to the ground like any manmade thing left too long near the unforgiving kiss of the sea. I had to live in the lighthouse itself now, a solid stone structure that towered up towards the heavens and wouldn't disintegrate for as long as I was alive. That's all that mattered.

I tugged up the corner of my mattress and took out my comforting stone, shaped like a tiny pillow, and the weight of it filled my palm, my heart, with a sense of peace. I pressed its worn curves to my hand and closed my eyes, cleared my mind.

"Show me Galo," I whispered to it.

At first, dark shadows spun over the stone, but then it focused, cleared, as if black waters had parted.

Galo had never been a handsome man, not even when I was little, when I stole the stone and started back in fright at his visage. He sat at a small table now and had his head in his hands. His long, tangled hair--white as foam--curled around his ears and down and over his back and chest.

Sometimes, lately, I pitied him.

There was no sound to accompany these pictures, so when his cottage door opened, when Nor entered to stand behind Galo, I gaped. Almost tenderly, she stepped forward and touched his shoulder with one fin-long hand.

He shrugged her off quickly, said something pointed. She drew away from him, mouth downturned, and left the room.

I put the stone away.

That night, I gathered my cloak about me, my grandmother's cloak, much patched and mended, and wandered out of the lighthouse into the star-soaked night. I went down to my own small shore and stood up on the trunk of a tree that the last storm had washed onto my island. I shielded my eyes against the grinning moon and watched the procession of the townspeople.

They came from their houses, from their shacks. Sometimes, when my mother told me the story of how Galo had made the town, forming it from mud, she smirked behind her hand, said, "He didn't know what a town was made of, so he shaped the houses based on glimpses he'd seen from the water. He didn't know how houses worked, what walls and windows were, so the sea people were left with cold floors and doors that would never open."

But I'd seen the insides of those houses, knew that this part of my mother's story wasn't quite right. Perhaps the townsfolk had gotten what they needed from other towns, trading fish or stories for chairs and bowls.

The people came now, trails of people, men and women, walking graceless and graceful in turns down to the edge of the sea in the harbor, a curved beach as smiling as the moon.

They gathered in a long line, one after the other, all turned toward me, but not really me. They were looking out to the sea, the ocean that could not embrace them, the water close but closed off to them.

They stood on the sand of the beach, and they did not move. They did not speak. The splash of the waves was nearly silent upon my little beach, and I watched the sea people, as I did every night. And they watched me.

The moon shifted overhead slowly.

I grew tired as sentinel and stepped down from the tree trunk. I went back inside, shut and locked the door as

I had done a hundred times before, a thousand times, and I put myself to bed while the sea people stood along the shoreline and stared, unmoving, at an untouchable sea.

I saw her before she stepped upon my sands this time. It was morning. Again, I checked the nets, mended the breaks, spun the magic to replace the strings that were too faded, did it all from the edge of the water, eyes closed, hands held out. Her little coracle bumped upon the edge of the beach, and I paused, opened my eyes, turned to take in her small shape as she dragged the boat up onto land. She moved like a girl now, truly, all hints of animal gone.

"Hello," said Nor, coming to greet me, smiling shyly, fingers held out. Today, I took her hand, felt the smooth skin brush against my calloused palm. She held on a bit too long, and then she dropped my hand awkwardly.

Still not human enough.

"Today…" she began, but I shook my head.

"No," I told her, as I would always tell her.

She nodded, still smiling, as if she'd expected my answer. "Is it all right if I eat with you? I brought lunch."

I opened my mouth, sighed, nodded.

We shared a quiche with bits of seaweed sprinkled throughout. I wrinkled my nose from time to time but ate my portion without saying anything, staring down at my hands and the small china plate, not up and across at my visitor, who ate her quiche with a knife and fork and had folded her napkin upon her lap.

"Are you ever lonely?" she asked. I didn't answer.

"You're brave," she said. "I would be very lonely."

I shook my head. I was lonely, and I wasn't

brave.

She leaned back in her chair, took in the roundness of the lighthouse, the scrubbed cupboards, the neatly made husk bed opposite the table. She got up, ran her fingers along the wood and stone, circled the room as I watched her with hooded eyes, nervous. Would her touch leave a lingering of her perfume? Her scent was not unpleasant, but it was distinct, different, and I was unaccustomed to different things.

"You live here all alone," she said.

I nodded.

"Did you grow up alone?"

I sighed. "I grew up with my mother. She died when I was fifteen."

"Was that hard?" She sat across from me with her wide, brown eyes, and I knew it was a genuine question. She was curious.

I cleared my throat. "In some ways, it was hard. In others, no."

This seemed to satisfy her, for she stood and gathered her things in her small, plain basket, brushing her fingers over mine when she reached to take my plate. I shuddered, but she seemed not to notice, and she smiled at me when I rose.

"It was lovely to talk to you. You are not a bad witch. I have decided that."

I was too stunned to reply until after she had left, the old door closing fast behind her.

"Thank you," I said.

"Show me Nor," I whispered to the stone, pressing my hands together. First, the stone showed me a muddy, distorted image. And then there she was.

She was laughing, throwing back her head and

laughing at something a tall, thin man had said. He was bent down almost double at the waist to whisper a word in her tiny, shell-shaped ear.

She was surrounded by people, and they all stood in Galo's house, the largest house in the town. There were rich tapestries draped over the walls and thick carpets upon the floor. I thought of my own humble furnishings—old and colorless—and drew my lips together.

He came striding down the staircase now. He was dressed in loose pants and a dirty white shirt. His hair rose around his head like a writhing creature. He said something to Nor. She sighed and shook her head, did not look the least bit afraid. I wondered if I would be afraid, confronted by that angry old god with teeth sharper than those of the shark men. He said something else, and the sea people backed away from Nor, but she simply shook her head again, folded her arms.

Galo turned and stood along the far wall, looking through a window. I could see the view through that window, knew it looked out upon the bay, and, past that, to my own island.

I covered the stone with my hands and put it away.

I drew water from the magicked well and washed my face in it. It was so cold, I shuddered, put my hands upon the well rim, stood for a long moment, letting the waves of chill pass through and away from me. The salt breeze was blowing from the north today, and my mother had often foretold omens by the wind's direction. North was ill tidings, always ill tidings, she'd whispered to me so many times, spinning a circle about herself as if it could protect her.

Nor came a second time that day, so my mother might have been right.

"I brought you dinner," she explained, not even greeting me but brushing past. I stood on the hillock before the shore, staring at her, open-mouthed. "Do you like biscuits?" she said. "I brought you biscuits and a good, fish gravy."

"My answer is still no," I told her, following after her, pressing my hands together to keep my fingers from shaking. "I will not ever answer his demands otherwise.'"

"I did not ask you to, did I?" She glanced up from setting my table, and her eyes were flashing, and her wide smile turned her lips up at the corners, almost teasing.

"Why else would you have come?"

"To keep you company," she replied, and spread a bright red-and-white checked cloth over the table. It hid the cracks and the smooth-scrubbed surface, made the room look almost cheerful.

"Come, sup with me," she said then.

I did.

That night, when I walked out to the shore, to my tree trunk, to my vigil, my thoughts chased after themselves in my head, and I almost tripped, climbing up the bark to stand at my usual, well-worn crook.

The dinner had been very good.

I shielded my eyes against the almost new moon, even though it shed too little light to truly obscure my vision. I watched the processional of sea people making its way down to the shore. They stood, one beside the other, all the way around the bay, and they raised up their faces to the scent of the surf and the stars, and they trained their eyes to the deep blue waters, and they did not move, did not speak, did nothing but stare with a longing I could almost understand.

This was the first night I found Nor among them.

I looked for her, but I was too far for faces. I felt Galo's presence at the center of the line, felt it because of his tie to my family and me. And there, beside him, was

Nor. I don't know how I knew her—not by sight—but I knew her, and she stood just as still and silent as her brothers and sisters, which surprised me, and I didn't really know why. I supposed I had expected her to be different from the others, for she was already different to me than all the others.

I dreaded the new moon. Tomorrow.

I did not sleep. I tossed and I turned, and--once or twice--I rose to peek out of my curtained window. The threadbare cloth did little to block the light during the day, or even during the night, if the moon was bright, but it made me feel secure in the fact that--no matter what--the lighthouse was shielded from the nighttime gazes of the sea people. I didn't know what I was afraid of, why my skin chilled when they made their nightly line and watched the ocean.

My mother's stories were loud in my head tonight, though, and I remembered how she said they waited and watched for weakness, waiting to destroy me so that they could set themselves free.

I was exhausted by morning.

"You do not look well," said Nor when she arrived, when she dragged her coracle up on the shore, met me at the edge of the grass and the sand. I sat, tiredly, my head in my hands, and when she bent down beside me, I did not move away from her, though she sat much too close, the warmth of her body hot against my leg.

When I made no reply, she handed me an apple, sun-ripened and hard, and a piece of thick, crumbly bread.

"Breakfast," she said, and did not look at me but, rather, back the way she had come, toward the town. I ate in silence.

With her hands clasped in her lap, her hair disheveled and tossed in whichever direction the wind teased it, she looked calm and content, though wild. I envied the townspeople sometimes, and I felt shame for that envy. She was prisoner to an old, forgotten god, kept from her home, probably never to see it again, and yet…the way she sat, poised, calm, clear like a full moon night, she seemed much happier than me, the witch who contained them all, the jailer with the magic key.

I could not finish my breakfast, dropped the half-eaten piece of bread to the ground as I rose. An angry gull swooped in, audacious enough to land beside Nor, and scooped crumbs down its gullet before either of us could protest. It took off with great sweeps of white wings and flew out to sea.

"They are despicable, vermin," I spat out, recognizing from some far, removed place that my mother had spoken the very same words in the very same voice.

"He was only hungry," said Nor, upturning her eyes to me, face drawn.

She left without asking the question.

Even though the moon was new, I could sense where it hung in the sky, suspended and ponderous, out of reach and dark to us. I shivered within my cloak, drew it closer about myself, as if I could bind safety to me with its worn, patched fabric. It smelled of seaweed and salt, fish and sweat, and it smelled like my grandmother and my mother, and I suppose that, now, it smelled of me. There was nothing to differentiate my scent from that of my mother's or my grandmother's, and that--for some reason-- filled my heart with alarm. I was already nervous from the moon's dark ascension in the sky, and when I climbed the tree trunk, waiting for the procession, my heart beat a rhythm that the waves could not drown.

The moon affected my powers but never so strongly as on the new and full nights. On the full moon, I was drunk from the energies. The shining net, suspended underwater, glowed so brightly that the entire bay shone from it. But on the new…

No living creature got past the nets. Save for on a new moon night.

Nor had come on the last new moon.

I rubbed my eyes tiredly, remembered the night, a month past, clear as glass, as if it were only a moment ago. I slept badly on the nights leading up to the new moon, tossing and turning as I thought about how best to keep my lineage's oath, how best to thwart Galo's plans. But the more I thought, the more I worried, and the more I worried, the worse I slept. And then, the night came, and I was exhausted and nervous and shaky and absolutely terrified that I would be the disappointment of my family, a line of women who had sacrificed their lives to a curse.

I didn't want to be a disappointment. So I did my best. But sometimes my best fell short. Like last month.

It had been such a cold, black night. A storm had kicked up during the afternoon, and when I came out to keep my vigil, the rain lanced down slantwise, and I could not see, save for the breaking waves. A slowly creeping mist hung suspended over the water.

The seal bolted through the net. I know that much but not how. She might have gotten spooked in the water. Maybe a shark chased her. But, however she did it, she came through, sliced through the silver strands of the net, and I crumpled when she did, for the net was tied to me like all other parts of the island. I cried out from the pain, hand over my heart, falling to my knees in the roar and rush of the gale. I could feel her, that seal, darting through the bay toward the shore, and I knew that Galo called to her. I did my best, in that biting rain, to repair the break, and I mourned the fact that yet another sea creature had lost its freedom.

My mother had told me that Galo called to the sea always and that all of its creatures wanted nothing more than to please him and answer his call. That's why it was so important to be vigilant, to never falter, to repair the nets whenever there was the mere whisper of a break. Every new creature that rose from the seas to be transformed by Galo was another nail in the coffin of humanity--a fact my mother had told me day in and day out. What she didn't say, but what was understood, was that every creature that got through the net was our responsibility, our failing.

Now another new moon had come. I had never let a creature through before, had never wavered enough to truly fail, until Nor. It had been a great failing. Galo was using her to get to me. I knew it. I scrubbed at my face, tried to peer through the mist.

Sometimes, I dreamed of what Galo must have been like before he assumed his human shape. The stories my mother had told me to frighten me were always fresh in my mind, dripping with dark water, clouding the bright days. I rubbed at my eyes again and climbed the tree trunk. My skin rose in gooseflesh, and I was chilled, strung taut like a bow and twice as tight.

Galo called to the sea creatures. He always called to the sea creatures. I glanced uneasily over my shoulder at the night, listened to the ever-present shush of waves on the side of the island that looked out to the sea. They battered the rocks there, the waves, the rocks that held up my lighthouse.

What if...what if Galo ever called up a monster? What if Galo called up something so gargantuan, so sinister, that no amount of magic could combat it, no net keep it out? What if the lighthouse, a massive structure, was dwarfed by its great bulk? What if it blocked out the stars—

I started so violently that I almost fell off of the tree when a loud splash sounded ahead of me in the mist. Fish often leapt up; sometimes dolphins came nosing around the bay, but my imagination traced dark grooves back to my worries and fears, and the hair upon my neck stood up. I felt myself quake.

I had been alone for so long that I never thought about what it was to be with someone, that reassurance of companionship that I would have, in that moment, given my heart for.

I heard it again.

This time, soft, small splashes came across the water, sounding eerie in the misty stillness. Oars. A boat. Someone had come from the town, at night, on a boat. This had never happened before.

The sea people, all of them, since the curse began, came together at night, along the beach. All night. Every night. It had never changed, was as dependable as the seasons spinning on or the moon waxing and waning. I climbed down from the tree, filled with dread. My mother had taught me that changes were never good. I had always believed her.

The coracle was shadowed in the wake of the mist, and when it edged up and onto my shore, I stared. Nor, small and sleek, leapt out of the boat, careful to keep her feet from the lapping waves, and dragged her small craft up further onto the sands.

"Hello," she said, quietly, staring up at me, eyes unblinking. "Good evening."

"What…" I said, and licked my lips, cleared my throat. I carefully folded my arms over my chest. "What are you doing here?"

She shrugged her shoulders, and, in the darkness, I could not see her expression. "I have been here a month now."

I watched her.

"Don't you ever want this to stop?" she whispered.

I was surprised by the question. I knew that there was no good answer to give her. Yes, I wanted it to stop.

Every day, I wanted it to *stop*. I wanted it to be *over*. Sometimes I thought about what it might have been like if I'd been born to another mother, if I had not been raised on an island to nurse a curse that was not my own. Sometimes I watched the seagulls and felt a welling of desire in me so fierce that it burned like a fire, a tongue of flame that licked my skin and spoke a single, sibilant word in my ear, over and over and over again: freedom.

Nor had not moved but simply gazed at me, hands clasped and folded before her, standing on the sands of my small, lonely beach.

"What are you doing to me?" I asked her. My voice cracked.

"Nothing," she said. I believed her.

I felt paralyzed. Should I invite her in? It was so cold, so wet out here in the dark and the mist. She had come all this way, and she hadn't said why, but there she stood, on my shore, small mouth closed, wide eyes searching mine. I stepped aside, held out one hand, pointing to my lighthouse.

"Come," I told her, and I ushered us both inside.

The night held a strange quality as she hung up her cloak over my cloak upon the peg, drawing out the chair she usually sat in, taking off her wet gloves. There was no fire in the grate because I had already banked it, but I set about asking it to wake up with a few bits of sea grass and a liberal push of magic.

"Do you use magic for everything?" she asked me, voice soft in the quiet of the lighthouse. I nodded, didn't look at her.

"I use it often." I fed the fire a handful of twigs.

"You keep the nets together." It was not a question.

"Yes."

"Why?"

I sat down upon the ground, turning a stick over

and over in my hands. I didn't know how to answer her question, felt broken as I tried to think of an answer. I didn't know why I kept up the curse that had been my grandmother's business, why I had listened to my mother's stories and believed them. But I had listened to them. I had believed them, that we were the last wall of goodness between a monster and the annihilation of the human race.

Sometimes, when I saw Galo in my stone, I laughed, put my hand over my mouth, held back a sob. He looked old, worn, tired--as far removed from a monster as a butterfly.

I could not express to Nor these crumpled feelings of rage and despair and pain. They ate up my heart from the inside, greedy jaws devouring all those things that made me myself, Meriel, and spitting out replications of my mother, my grandmother, instead.

So I sat on the floor, and I twisted the stick in my fingers, and I said not a word.

I heard a scrape of wood against wood and looked up just as Nor rose from her chair, as she sank down on the floor beside me.

She was too close. She smelled of salt and soft things. She reached across the small divide between us and took my hand, touched my rough skin with her new, smooth fingers, held my palm in her own as she drew it close, into her lap.

I stared, unable to move. She held my hand tight and close. Her face was hidden by a wave of long, brown hair that swept down and in front of her eyes, concealing her from me. She was so small, so fragile. The fire crackled far, far away as I took in the seal girl's slight form, the arch of her round shoulder under the cheap gray cloth.

"I have decided," she said, words so low, I could almost not hear them, "that we are both prisoners."

"I'm not a—" I began but stopped myself, bowed

my head. I did want to lie.

"Don't you ever wish…" she whispered, and she looked up, glanced at me quickly, wildly, and I saw the tears tracing down her cheeks, leaving a groove of silver upon her skin. "Don't you ever wish that it was all over? That things were the way they might have been…if this had never happened?"

I did.

I closed my hand in her lap to form a fist. She dropped her fingers away from me, and I drew back my limb, cradled it close to my chest as if it had been poisoned. I could not look at her. If I looked at her, I would lose my nerve, and I could not lose my nerve.

"You're trying to get me to say yes to him. It won't work."

"That's not—"

"You're all alike," I said, surprised at the words tumbling out of my mouth. *My* mouth, my mother's words. "Deceitful. Treacherous. You're all alike, and I will not yield to you."

A small part of myself, a lost, lone part, cried out from the dark within me as she rose.

"What part of you thinks this is right?" she asked me then, and I could hear the tears in her voice but dared not look up at her. "What part of you, Meriel?"

I pointed toward the door, terrified that, if I spoke, I would speak the truth.

The door crashed against the frame when she slammed it behind her. I waited until enough time had passed, until I felt certain her coracle had entered the cold and empty bay. Then, when I knew she had gone, I whispered it into the air, because I could not keep it inside of me any longer.

"No part of me," I told Nor's ghost, and I sat, hollow, beside the dying fire.

That had been too close. I needed to strengthen my resolve, my spells, my promise to my mother.

I had no choice. I must do a Calling.

The amount of energy necessary to do a Calling, the amount of magic I would need to spin, was gargantuan. To attempt such a thing on the day after the new moon was lunacy. But I couldn't think about that. I had no choice. I must.

I gathered bits of dried sea grass from the edge of the beach the next morning, and I waited for Nor to come. But she did not. I sat along the beginning of the sand, and I twisted the grasses together nervously and waited. I was disappointed when she did not appear. Which was mad, a mad reaction, and I knew that. When the sea grasses had been braided together, when I rose and made my way back to the lighthouse, I felt relief and pain wash over me.

It was good that she had not come. And, despite myself, I was sad that she hadn't.

I built up the fire, laying my braided grasses in a special pattern in the flames. When all was ready, I drew a circle about myself with chanted words and gestures, and I sat in its center.

"Grandmother," I spoke into the cool calm of the lighthouse. "Come to me."

She came.

I had spoken to my grandmother once before. My own mother had done a Calling when I was small, for the nets had broken nearly beyond her ability to repair, and she needed counsel. What I remembered from that exchange, from my first sight of the woman who was the cause of all of this, was that she was smaller than I had imagined she would be. Shouldn't she have been tall, huge, a wall of power? But, no, she was stooped, and her eyes were rheumy, even in death.

She came now, and she had not changed from the vision of my memory. She stood leaning on the ghost of a cane. I could see through her, see the crackling flames behind her. She cast about, took in the state of the lighthouse, likely wondered why I was performing the spell here, rather than within the now-ruined cottage, and she shook her head.

"Why have you summoned me, girl?"

"I needed advice," I replied guardedly, and I realized as I spoke those words that I did not want advice from my grandmother. What could I tell her? That my resolve was weakening, that the curse was weakening, because of a beautiful girl?

That was it, wasn't it? When I closed my eyes, I saw Nor's face. When I dreamed, I dreamed of her, and when she had not come that morning, I felt a small part of myself shriveling up, growing small...dying.

My grandmother watched me work my jaw with an impassive face. "Well? Spit it out, girly," she said at last, though not unkindly. I folded my hands in my lap and stared down at my fingers.

"A seal got through the net."

"It's bound to happen." She shrugged wearily, closing her eyes. "Did you kill it?"

"Kill it?" I choked out. I shook my head, eyes gaping. "No..." I couldn't fathom such a thing. With a pang, I realized I could not fathom my existence without Nor.

"That's what you must do, when they enter the bay. Better to die, make a meal for you, then serve Galo, trapped forevermore. That's not an existence we would wish on our worst enemies." She spoke to me as she'd spoken to my mother: imperious, as if a child sat before her, not a grown woman with her own mind.

I watched my grandmother for a long moment, and I found I could feel nothing but disgust for her. "Be gone,"

I whispered, and when she opened her mouth, outraged, she vanished. She'd been about to scold me, surely. Call me weak-hearted, just as she'd called my mother. I remembered that now.

I put my head in my hands and breathed steadily for several long moments. I was so tired.

A knock at the door.

I sat, frozen, fear moving through my blood like ice.

Again, there it was—a knock at the door.

I rose, mouth open. I didn't know what to do.

Knock, knock, knock.

I opened the door.

She stood there, eyes wide and brown and beautiful, staring up at me as if she had never left. Her mouth was set in a firm, hard line, and she did not smile like before.

"He made me come," she said simply, "to ask the question. Will you take his offer, Meriel?"

I stared past her to the meadow, to the beach, to her little coracle on the sand. I took her by the wrist and drew her inside.

We stared at one another for a long moment, and I knew I was much too close to her, breathing in the salt of her, the warmth of her. She leaned against the door and looked up at me through thick lashes, pressing her fingers against the wood my grandmother had lashed together to form a gateway through which I could never escape.

"You," I said, and licked my lips, closed my eyes. "You're making me want you. With magic."

She sighed, then, breathed out, and I looked at her. Her own eyes shone; there were tears there. I watched them fall.

"I am not bewitching you. How could I bewitch a witch?" she whispered back. "Maybe this has nothing to do with magic, Meriel."

"You're magic," I told her, and when the words had left my mouth, I knew how true they were, how deeply true. She was magic to me, the sort of spell I could never make, could never understand.

She stepped forward. It was tentative, uncertain, when she put her hands up through the space between us, drew them around my neck as if I might be easily broken and she did not wish to break me. She leaned against me, and tilting on her tiptoes, she pressed her mouth to mine.

Her lips were salty, her tongue hot and smooth and soft, and I realized my hands were upon her waist long after I had placed them there. Heat rushed through me, and I felt my toes upturn, and then I stepped forward, pressing her to me, wrapping my arms around her so tightly that her breath rushed out, and she laughed a little against my mouth, a laugh of delight, deep and soft. I loosed my arms, gentle, then, and I pressed my lips against hers, my tongue against hers, and our teeth clicked. I was graceless, desperate, and when I shoved her against the bulk of the door, picked up her leg, put my hand beneath her bottom, I heard a sound like a whine, a sad, pathetic thing that gusted from my own lungs. I was starved, and she knew it, and she loved it, for her lips raked my skin, and her tongue trailed down my neck, and her hands were suddenly sharp as her nails scratched down my back when I pressed her harder against the wood, fumbling with my fingers, uncertain how to revere something so lovely.

"Here," she said, and she took my hand, closed her fingers around mine, and guided my palm up and along her thigh where her skin was hot and soft and wet. I closed my eyes, and I stopped. Every thing that I was strained against the pause, crying out, screaming and roaring within me. She stopped, too, and I heard our breath between us, sharp and short and hard.

"What is it?" she whispered, haltingly, but she knew. I knew.

67

"I can't do this," I told her, and I gritted my teeth, satisfied to feel pain thunder up and through my skull, bringing a red clarity.

Still, I did not move my hand.

"Why can't you?" she asked, panting against me. She moved her body, brought her hips down upon my fingers, brushed her lips against my jaw. "There is no law against this. This does not break the curse. Everything you do remains safe, Meriel. This will not damn you."

And then, she whispered, "Please."

When I closed my eyes, I saw my grandmother's disapproving face; my mother's weak, bitter one; the sad line of sea creatures stretched along the shore; the way that Galo held his head in his hands every afternoon and remained still, for hours, in despair. When I closed my eyes, I saw my long, lonely years of monotony, the times that I fell asleep listening to the roar of the sea and the wind and wishing for... I didn't even know what I wished for sometimes. Other times, I did know, and there was a drumming of blood within me that called for something I could never attain. Freedom.

I closed my eyes, and when I did, this all flashed by in an instant. And when I opened them again, there she was, in front of me, in my arms, bare skin against my hand, eyes wide and beautiful and wild and not the least bit human. She was a monster, I was a monster, and when I bent my head and kissed her again, tasting the salt of an ocean that was prison and home to us both, I forgot everything else but that kiss, but Nor.

It didn't matter. Nothing mattered, and when we found the bed, when I pressed down on top of her and in her and for her, our blood rushed with the same pull of tide and shore, and when she cried out, I cried out. The wind that roared and whipped the sea up into a frenzy carried our voices away into the great nothingness of blue.

I changed.

I became something that did not yet have a name. I felt, for the first time, the only time, that I was important.

At dark, she said my name, kissed my neck, bowed beneath me.

I did not know what love felt like, had never known. I wondered if I knew it now.

She left my bed that night. I woke with the shifting of the thin mattress, watched her in the dark as she gathered up her underthings, her skirt, her blouse, and put them on slowly. She left the cottage without looking back at me, and I followed her.

Nor went down to the edge of the sea, her small form bright beneath the tiniest fragment of moon that hung in the sky, suspended. She straightened herself at the shore, stood tall and unbending. I watched the mass of sea people on the bay's edge, watched as she looked to them, as they looked to her, as the only sound that roared about us was the sing of water and wind and the howling of an approaching storm.

I walked across the meadow, drawing on my nightgown, shivering in the cold. I stood beside Nor.

"Why do you do this?" I asked her. For my entire life, and long before, the sea people had stood facing the ocean in silence all night, every night.

Nor said, "Because we must."

She stared at the water and offered me no more words.

"But why must you, Nor?" I asked her, and I reached out and touched her arm.

"Because we miss it," she whispered so quietly.

Together, we stared at the ocean, and I felt myself unraveling.

"Then you should go back. Step into the water

and—"

"I won't abandon him." Her eyes flashed. "I came here of my own choosing, as did we all. To help him. To stand with him. To save him, if we can."

"To save him…" I repeated her words, marveled at the weight of them. "I thought he forced you—"

"No. We chose this. As you, Meriel, have also chosen." Her voice trembled, and she lowered her gaze to the shifting sand at our feet.

"I have never thought of it as a choice, Nor. I don't know why I do…what I do," I said then, gulping down air, squeezing my eyes shut against the pain before me and within me.

"We all do what we feel we must," she said gently.

In the dark, she moved her hand until it was in mine, curling her fingers about my own.

"It's been three days," she said when she kissed me. "I can feel him. He's calling me back."

"Don't go," I whispered, swallowed. "Please don't go."

"I cannot ignore his summons." She traced her fingers along my collarbones, down my ribs, over my hips. I shivered and moved closer to her, pillowing my head over her heart.

"When will you return?" I asked her, curling my fingers about her waist, feeling her pulse beat beneath my skin.

"Soon," she said, and she kissed my eyes, my nose, my mouth, my heart.

Nor rose, dressed, left the cottage. I lay on the mattress, crippled, unable to breathe. When she left, I felt myself leaving, felt some piece of me remove itself and launch out upon the waters.

I had not tended the nets for three days. I remembered that—no, I was well aware of that—and I raked my fingers through my hair, put on a clean shift, climbed out of bed.

The nets had at least twenty small breaks, but none large enough to permit an animal to pass through. I stared at the sea for a very long time. I called up the magic, but I was frustrated as I began to slowly make the repairs. Angry. I did not want to do this thing, this chore. I hated it; I hated it passionately, deeply, and I broke away from the energies, felt them ricochet about and finally lodge into a small boulder at the edge of the water.

Disgusted, I turned away and stalked back indoors.

"Show me Nor," I whispered to my stone. I knelt beside the bed, and I waited.

She was in Galo's house, and she sat beside him. He lay on the thick carpet before the empty fireplace. I stared in horror.

The old man wept, wept piteously, burying his face in her lap as she stroked his hair and stared ahead, eyes empty, blank, though she wept, too.

I threw the stone away from me, heard it breaking as it hit the lighthouse wall, shattering into tiny pieces that could never be magicked back together. I breathed out and put my face in my hands, and I felt my body shaking.

"I don't know what to do," I wailed, and the words sounded broken. They were taken up by the wind that whistled through the open door, carried out and away from me, over the open sea. "I don't know what to do," I whispered then, and I kept the words close. They whirled about me as I stood, as I hugged myself, as I paced the floor of the lighthouse over and over and over again, feeling the familiar wood beneath my bare feet, feeling the grooves I knew by heart beneath my toes and then my knees, when I knelt down again beside my bed, pressed my fingers to the sheets, to the threadbare blanket that had covered us both, Nor and me.

If I left.

If I left…

If I…left.

I would never see Nor again.

Galo would shatter the curse, would call up his sea army, would destroy the world.

I would break my mother's heart. My grandmother's heart. *I* would destroy the world.

Wouldn't I?

I spread my fingers over the sheets, counted them as I had when I was a child. One, two, three, four, five… I swallowed and pressed them harder against the mattress, so hard I felt it creak beneath me as I stood up, as I drew my hands together, as if in prayer.

But I wasn't sorry, and I wouldn't pretend I was.

I turned, and I left the lighthouse, standing uncertain at the edge of the beach.

"First, he'll set fire to the world, burn the crops, bring diseases," my mother had said, and I heard her voice in the wind now, the damnation, all the stories she'd spun for me when I was little, the nightmares I had had each night feeding off of her words. "He will laugh as man dies. He has no pity."

I had seen him weep.

"They are monsters," she'd told me over and over and over again, making me repeat it until my tongue was tired.

Wasn't I a monster, too?

I rubbed my shoulders, and then I took a step forward. I felt the magic settle about me as I pulled and pulled.

And then, before me, there was Nor's coracle, summoned by my spell, bobbing empty up and down at the edge of the water.

I stood in the sand. I felt the tide come up and touch my bare feet, felt it run over my skin, so cold. I let out my breath in a hiss.

I closed my eyes, balled my hands into fists, and I stumbled into the boat, feeling my feet leave land for the first time…in my life.

I took the oar and clumsily pushed off from the shore, even as I began to hear the breaking behind me. I heard the scream of stone against stone, and I did not look back, but I saw the tall shadow of the lighthouse in the water as it began to sway, back and forth, back and forth, and it was falling apart, crumbling. The roar surrounded me as I paddled, and the storm that had hovered hit at last as I felt the spell shatter, as the lighthouse fell down, as the net began to unravel.

I paddled as the rain hit, paddled hard when the swells began to grow, tossing the coracle back and forth, filling it with water and emptying it in the same heartbeat. I gritted my teeth, and I pushed against the sea as the last wisps of the net unwound themselves, as I felt the net vanish. The roar of the wind and the howl of the sea surrounded me, and I wept in the salt water, in the rainwater, my tears mingling with all of the water, water everywhere.

Somehow, eventually, I reached the shore. The sea people were gathered there, and they stared at me with open mouths as my boat pitched itself upon the sand. I fell as I climbed out, felt the solidity of sand and land beneath my hands and let out a great wail that was lost in the bellow of the people as they raised their heads to the sky, to the great, gathered storm clouds, and threw up a cheer that dwarfed the music of the storm.

And then, Nor.

She ran down the shore, her eyes wide, wild, and she helped me rise, her hands soft against my skin. Always so soft. Tears streaked down her long nose, and

73

when she kissed me, she tasted of their salt. Galo appeared behind her. He was skeletal, a shadow, and he stared at me with haunted eyes.

One by one, the sea people began to walk into the water.

Galo brushed past me, limping, and when he entered the sea, as the white foam dripped over his legs, he let loose a cry of pain. But then he sank below the water, was consumed by the water, and was gone, but I saw something large and dark moving through the bay, just below the surface.

I couldn't breathe.

But then I looked at Nor, and she took my hand, and she kissed it. She stood with me for a long moment, but it was not long enough, would never be long enough.

She mouthed two words before she turned and embraced the water with her brothers and sisters—people who had never belonged here; people I had watched in my stone, watched mourning the sea night after night; people who were not people—now going home.

What Nor said was, "Thank you."

SEEK

She tasted of salt. My lips stung against the back of her hand, her gleaming skin cold and wet from the sea.

A moment ago, she'd risen from the waves like a dark, dripping goddess, and now her eyes met mine with a knowing expression. I waited, eager.

Because I had tasted of her, would I become rich in knowledge? Isn't that how the old stories go? One bite, one kiss, one taste, and innocence—ignorance—is lost forever.

She stepped from the sea, her feet light upon the sand, water rushing to meet the backs of her ankles as I offered her a hand, felt her smooth fingers glide between my rough ones.

"Why have you summoned me?" Her voice was hushed, cool and liquid, unblemished by human emotion. I fell to my knees, because beneath her words was a lulling power, like the tide, hissing below a body, dragging it down and down into the blue.

Shouldn't it be obvious? I thought but did not ask. *Shouldn't it be obvious why one invokes a muse?*

When she licked her lips, then, coral-red tongue

moistening a too-wide grin, I spied a pointed tooth, like a shark's, within the shell-pink mouth.

I should not have come here.

My hands clawed at the sand.

"I need your help," I said, because I was stupid, or I was brave, and, in any case, I was desperate. "I need a muse's touch."

"Ah," she breathed out, and, crouched down beside me, eyes wide, unblinking, she took me in as if I were something to devour. Even as she squatted beside my kneeling form, she was taller, larger, hair streaming over her wet shoulders like waterweed. "You need me," she said, and I shuddered because the words were sharp coming out of her mouth, like broken glass from a sunken ship, cutting. I knew what she meant when she said, "You need me," and I am certain she knew that I knew: *You are powerless without me.*

I should have risen. I should have turned and—without looking back—gone from the water's edge, from her. She was bound to the water, held in its thrall, unable to overcome the susurration of wave and gull, and I could have moved away from her sharp, dripping fingers, her wet wicked mouth.

But I needed her. And so I stayed.

"Help me," she said, after grinning, after tapping her chin with one long curved nail, considering me. "Help me out of the water, and all you ask for will be yours. And more," she murmured, leaning toward me, leering. "So much more."

I did press back, then, against the boulder behind me. Like a sea serpent, she crouched, coiled, watching me with hooded eyes, never ceasing her smile. She was not beautiful, but her eyes snagged me. I flailed beneath their gaze, a fish on a hook.

"You've kissed me once," she whispered, holding out her hands to me, her hands with fingertips that trickled upon the sand—blue drops, white drops, flashing in the almost-setting sun. "Kiss me twice, and I am loosed from this cursed edge, and then I can help you, give you what you want. So. Kiss me again." She paused, cocking her head so quickly, I heard a bone snap within her. "But first… Tell me—what is your name?"

I exhaled a slow, jerky breath, swallowed. The sorceress had warned me of this: "Do not give her anything you do not wish her to possess," she'd said. "For she *will* possess it, any gift given to her."

The sorceress, Mariana, had pressed her finger against my lips when I opened my mouth, when I began to ask, "But what of mine could she hope to possess?"

She'd set her lips along my neck, my jaw, my own mouth, then, and whispered, "Your heart, of course. Your soul."

I had laughed against her kiss. What was mine would remain mine. No one could take anything from me that I did not wish to give. I was quick, and I was invincible, and I was learning from the most powerful sorceress how to subdue a muse.

I would not fail.

"Kiss me once more, lovely woman," said the muse, raising her nose to peer down at me. "Kiss me, and you will have all you desire."

"I…" I coughed, cursing myself for the unsteadiness in my voice. "I have battled against many monsters, and I have defeated them all."

She cocked her head, measuring me up. Her mouth curved deeper, amused. She did not believe me, and shame rose, burning my cheeks. "I am clever," I insisted. "I do not need to be strong." Her unfeeling eyes roved my body, my arms and legs. I flexed my hands, nails biting into my palms. What did I care for this creature's opinion of me? But my face was hot, and I breathed out, huffing into the salted air beneath the dying sun.

"Why do you tell me these things, these boasts? Of what consequence are they to me?" She held out her arms, fingers widespread, and her eyes flashed. "Kiss me!"

"I tell you," I whispered, pressing my back against the solidity of the boulder, worn smooth by the waves, "because I did it all for love. For a woman, I have beheaded the Elesis Giant, and for a woman, I have tamed the fire mares. And for a woman, I have come to you."

"And what would you have of me?" she whispered back, sinking lower and lower into the water, eyes dark.

"For a woman, I must now spin a tale. The last of my endeavors, if her father will let me have her." I took a deep breath. "It must be the most beautiful tale that the king has ever heard. And I am no storyteller." I looked down at my hands, at my fingers, as I pressed my palms together. "So I had to find a muse, a muse to give me a story."

"Ah, yes. The young, pretty hero," she murmured between the rush of the ocean waves, "come for a tale from the old, ugly muse."

I gaped in astonishment. As she spoke, as she spent the final syllables, shadows crept over her face, distorting it, elongating some features, shriveling others. Her hands sank into the lapping water.

I shook my head, resolute. "I have called you up, and you must fulfill my wish," I told her sternly, firmly. "I know the rules, the ancient laws."

"You will come again tomorrow," said the muse, her skin taking on the bluish-gray of the water, as if the color had risen from the slick surface and stained her flesh. "You will come again tomorrow," she repeated, "and I will tell you a story."

Defying the spells, the magic, the *rules*, the muse drew back and away from me and dove into the water, sinking without a ripple into deep nothingness. Gone.

I buried my head in my hands, howled, screamed, tore at my hair and kicked the boulder. My fury was so absolute, reason proved impossible to find. Finally, I staggered on trembling legs away from the water, mounted Dana, my worried mare, and rode her back to the sorceress's cave.

"You *lied*," I roared when I reached the cave mouth, pausing beneath the jagged stone teeth that jutted overhead. The air seeping from the cave's depths was cool and musty, and it carried to me the melody Mariana played upon her harp.

"Did you hear me?" I stomped my foot against the rocks. "You lied!"

The music ceased, and a moment later, Mariana stood before me.

"What is this talk of lying?" Her mouth twisted into an indulgent smile. "Did you not find the muse? Was she not compliant to your wish?"

I stood, shaking, at the entrance to the cave and stared at Mariana, beautiful creature that she was, with hair as black as a starless night—shining, shining—and skin as lustrous as a copper vessel. I tore at my hair again, and I raged and groaned as she laughed behind her hand, and then she reached out to me, head tilted, mouth teasing and soft.

"Come, brave knight, lovely lady," she whispered as I quieted and drew close, a petulant child enfolded in her arms. "I suspect you will fare better tomorrow."

"How did you know? How did you know she told me to come back?" I asked her, pulling away even as her arms encircled my waist, tugged at my belt with its golden buckle.

"Because the muse does things in threes, dearest," she whispered into my ear, drawing my head down to her quick, red mouth, kissing me sweetly once upon my cheek, once upon my chin, and then, deeply, upon my lips. "You will not get your story tomorrow, either. So," she said, pressing a finger to my mouth as I began to protest, "you must beseech her for three days. That is simply how these things are done."

"Oh, give me a battle, a foe, a sword," I growled, shaking my head, gouging at my eyes with the heels of my hands. "How I despise riddles, protocols, knotty steps of spells." I flung my arms wide, took in the sorceress's cave, her tidy shelves of potion bottles and earthen pots, the lanterns glowing with flameless fire.

"Spend the night with me, lady knight," she whispered, twining her arms about my neck, urging my face down again as she captured my mouth in a kiss. "Spend the night with me, and I will give you a word to appease the muse with tomorrow." Her fingernails trailed over my cheek. "Spend tomorrow night with me, and I will give you the toy that will bend her will to yours."

"You did lie," I said flatly, frowning as I gazed into her beautiful eyes. "You told me that today, the potion, the spells... You said that was all I needed."

"To *begin* it," she said easily, curling her fingers around my shoulders, petting my forehead lightly with a soft, sweet-smelling hand. "Two more days, and you will have what you came for, and you will go back to your precious *beauty*," she murmured, the last word hard, sharp. "Give me two more nights," she breathed, her mouth hot against my neck, her lashes fluttering there as I shivered. "Two more nights, and you will have your wish."

I sighed as she smiled prettily up at me, mouth curling up at the corners wide and full. "Now," she sighed, sinking her fingers into my hair, twining it again and again and again, "you have not told me your name. Tell it to me so that I may whisper it back to you." She leaned against me, lips nearly touching mine.

"My name is Seek," I told her, as she kissed me,

as her mouth found the line of my jaw, the arch of my neck, and paused before my lips.

"Seek," she whispered in a breathless, singsong way. "*Seeeek*," she whispered again, her tongue tasting me as I exhaled, closing my eyes, finding the darkness of a night sky torn with stars.

Seek.

All of this was for my Lady Ella.

She was the most beautiful woman in the kingdom. Her hair was long and black and curling, and she wore it in countless braids, lovingly twined over her head and brow. Her skin smelled of fine oils and was the color of obsidian, rich and polished. Her voice was music, her smile warmth and star-shine, and there were none to compare to her. To win such a perfect creature's love would be worth any great effort, and my Lord Raul, the sovereign of our fair kingdom and her doting father, decreed that only the finest suitor would have his daughter's hand. And so I came this far and have done these things because Ella must love me above all other suitors, because *I* must be the one to win her.

That we had not yet *spoken* was but a minor detail. Her father commanded three very specific tasks, and I had completed all but one of them. And Ella nodded and smiled at me when I told the king of my commitment to the quest, of my ambition to marry his daughter. Ella had no cause to speak in that moment. When we did speak, Ella and I, I felt certain it would be a dulcet hour of perfection that I would, forevermore, cherish.

For she was so beautiful, and she was so lovely, and she would be mine.

Reclining upon Mariana's bed, I closed my eyes and saw Lady Ella's perfect face. When I opened my eyes, I saw Mariana's face—lovely, too, but not *as* lovely. And as Mariana kissed me, over and over, gazing at me with curving mouth and sparking eyes, I sighed a little and turned away.

"What is the matter, Seek?" she whispered, examining me as her hair hung down and brushed against my skin. "What do you desire? Name it." The whisper was soft, smooth; it trailed around me like a ribbon.

"I desire the end to my quest," I said simply, peevishly. I propped myself up on my elbow, and she slid off of me, running her hands through her long black hair, fingers deftly parting and reparting it as I watched its shimmering silk catch the dancing light.

"The end to your quest is a woman, is it not?" Mariana asked then, glancing at me sidelong, tongue flicking out between her lips to lick them. "Am I not a woman here before you, willing to fulfill your every longing?"

"You're beautiful," I agreed sullenly, sighing again, "but my Lady Ella—"

"Oh," she said, the word full and round. "Of course."

She rose off of the bed, sliding across the satin until her bare feet touched stone, and her hips swayed from side to side as she dove into a silken robe.

"The sun is slipping," she observed, crossing to the towering cabinet of pretty, sparkling bottles. She lingered there for a long moment, hand grazing one of the bottles, eyes closed, lips moving in a silent murmur. Then she picked up the bottle and returned to the side of the bed. At arm's length, she handed me the small glass vessel.

"Take this to the water's edge and call the muse as you did before," she whispered, crouching down as I turned the bottle this way and that in my hands. "Give her the bottle and repeat your request." Her eyes regarded me coolly, flat and dull. "And then, tomorrow, you will win your prize."

"What is in this thing? Why would she want this?" I asked, but the sorceress shook her dark head, smiling, indulgent again.

"Ah, Seek, patience. You will see," she murmured, kissing my brow.

The muse came as before, wary, her legs scaled this time, hands dripping, fingers long and boneless, eyes black as ink and shining. She looked different, diminished, less than she had been the day before, but I still knew her, and she knew me, too, as she moved along the water's edge, pacing on her hands and knees like a chained cur.

"I will not give you a story, hero."

"You must, and you will." My words were made of stone. The sorceress had told me that the muse could command the elements, that she possessed great power, but she looked harmless, pathetic, as she skulked the line where sea met shore, crawling and panting in the twilit sun.

"Here," I told her, as one might speak to a bawling child, doll in hand. I held out the bottle, and she paused in her obsessive pacing to watch me with unblinking eyes.

"What have you brought me?"

I shook the vessel, impatient. "I was not told what it is, only that you will like it." I lay the bottle flat on my palm. "Come along now. Take it."

The muse eyed me for a long moment, sniffing the air. Then, with surprising quickness, she snatched the bottle, watching my face as her fingers drew the glass vessel toward her. She uncorked the bottle with a deft thumb, and she poured the contents of it out onto her hand.

Sand. It was filled with sand that drifted over her hand, mounding, swirling. I stared as the sand and her skin spelled out a single word; it faded too quickly for me to read. Then the last sparkling bits trickled through the spaces between her strange fingers, down into the sea.

"Thank you," she said, dropping cork and bottle upon the edge of the beach. "What a lovely gift."

The strength seemed to drain from her then, and she sank down into the water as the sun, too, sank into the waves, abandoning the sky. "Come again tomorrow, and you will have your wish." Without a splash, she dove beneath the waves.

I wanted to ask her what had happened, what the gift, as she called it, had been, but, in truth, I did not care. I rubbed my palms together, grinning. That had been simple! Tomorrow, I was certain, would prove even easier. As I mounted Dana, I gave a cheerful shout and raised my fist in the air.

Soon, the beautiful, beloved Lady Ella would be my bride.

"It happened just as you said it would," I told Mariana, gleeful, as I pulled off my boots and dropped them beside the hearth. I massaged my ankles and leaned back to rest my head against the hand-carved chair. "Tomorrow she'll give me the story. Tomorrow I go home to my darling Ella—triumphant! At last, I shall marry the princess!" I rose and paced the room, my hands latched behind my back. "I've already planned what I will wear in the wedding." I smiled smugly. "I'll wear my best suit of armor, shined up like a mirror. Oh, I realize it's a bit out of fashion to wear armor to a wedding, but it looks so fine, so impressive—"

"Yes," said Mariana, not glancing up from the

weaving on her lap, pale rushes forming the beginnings of a basket bowl. "You will look fine in armor. Very fine. And you have told me how beautiful Ella is, I believe, lady knight, a hundred times." She looked at me, then, brows raised, mouth smiling, though the smile did not touch her eyes. "But tell me this: what is your lady *like*?"

"Why, I've told you. She…Well, she is *beautiful*," I finished, with a chuckle. "I'm not certain what you're asking—"

"Oh, Seek." Mariana tilted her head back and laughed. "Is she amusing, pray? Does she tell good jokes? Is she good in bed, lady?" she asked me, her eyes and words sharp. "Is she kind to children? What books does she like to read? What hobbies does she while away her dreary days with, seated beside her father as she stares across the same hall she's stared across every hour of her life, chained like a prized beast to a pretty, bejeweled chair?"

I blinked and stared, mouth agape. I had no answers to these questions, did not know what to say in response, so I held my tongue.

Mariana nodded. "As I thought." She peered down at the weaving in her hands. And then she said, softly, sweetly, "You know, my dear, there is more to a woman than her pretty face."

I snorted a little and sat up straight. "You insult me, sorceress. How dare you tell a woman what there is to a woman?"

"It just seems," she said, twisting a reed over her fingers, "that you have become enamored with your princess for her appearance alone."

"That is not…" I paused, faltered. "Not *entirely* true. Everyone knows that my Lady Ella is unsurpassed in kindness and accomplishments and—"

"Tell me," said Mariana, eyes flashing. "You are a knight, are you not?"

"Indeed," I muttered, clenching my fists. "I have conquered the fiercest creatures in this kingdom. I have brought back five dragon heads, and I have—"

"Might I be correct in assuming that you have *fallen in love* with the dear Lady Ella for her status? That, if you marry this divine, perfect creature—as you have called her repeatedly—you will become the ruler of the kingdom, and that will be the final feather in your very feathered cap?" Her mouth smiled as she spoke, but her eyes burned, and her face hardened, and her hands tore at the reeds in her lap.

"Yes," I said, nose turned up, voice hot.

"The fact that you do not truly *love* Lady Ella is of no concern to you?"

I fell against the chair as if struck. "Mariana," I growled, a warning in my tone.

"Have I not spoken the truth?" She gazed at me, gazed deep into my eyes, unblinking. Something strange happened then, as if the cave walls moved in closer, or perhaps Mariana herself moved, because everything around me seemed to tilt and spiral… I clutched my head, dizzy.

But then all was still again. My light-starved eyes were playing tricks on me, surely. I rubbed at them with the heels of my hands.

"You know nothing of love," said Mariana, voice very small as she stared toward the cave opening. "That much is obvious. You do not know about love because you have never been *in* love. And I assure you, Seek, that love is something you *know*, once you discover it. It fills you, your bones, your body, and you are light and heavy, all at once, for you are consumed by it. Like a fire," she whispered. "Love is much like a fire. It devours you. Utterly. Have you ever been devoured, Seek?" she asked, her eyes black and deep and wide. I stared into them, unable to glance away. "To be devoured," she whispered, "is delicious. To be devoured—that's beauty."

"You speak," I murmured, voice trembling, "as a woman who has known love quite intimately."

"Ah," she sighed, smiling, staring down at the unfinished basket in her hands as if it held a secret. "Yes. Yes, that is true."

I ran my hands over my face, shaking my head. "And who was the fair damsel of your heart?"

"Fair?" she whispered, tilting her head. "Oh, no, you mistake me, Seek. She was not fair. And she was not," she laughed a little, breathy, "a damsel. She was a *force,* an element." Mariana's eyes bored through me. "I love her still, with my whole heart," she whispered. The strength behind those words was startling. I sat very still for a long moment.

"She is yet alive?" I asked her finally.

"Oh, yes."

"Then why are you not with her?"

She put her basket on the floor and stood, shook out her skirts in sharp, jerky movements, hands curled like claws against the fabric.

"That is no concern of yours, lady knight," she said, and then she knelt down before me, baring her legs, all soft-edged again and smiling. "This is the last night, and tomorrow... Tomorrow, you will get what you..." She chuckled a little. "What you *seek.* But tonight, my darling, you are mine."

"I am not yours," I said quickly, frowning, but she twined her hands in my hair, undoing the bow at my neck, pressing her skin against mine as she climbed into my lap, kissing and caressing and biting with sharp little teeth.

"And you," she breathed, leaning back after a long, agonizing, lovely moment. She breathed hard, mouth open. I watched her lips, her mouth, bound as if by a spell. "You must tell me, pretty Seek," she said, tracing her fingers over my shoulders and my neck, curling them into the hair at the base of my skull. "Is winning Ella your greatest dream?"

It was a surprising question, and I froze for a moment, staring up at her as she grinned down at me, moving herself against me, so warm and so soft. I shook my head. "No," I told her, astonishing myself. "It is not my greatest dream."

"What is, pretty Seek?"

"I want to rule the kingdom," I confessed, my tongue wagging a truth I had never voiced in my entire life. "I want to rule the kingdom, and when people speak of me, I want them to know that I am good and just and that I have the most beautiful woman of all at my side. I want them to fear me, and I want them to love me, and I want the rulers of all of the other kingdoms to know that they must never cross me. I want to be powerful," I told her, words spilling out of my mouth like water, rushing, running, flooding, "and I want to be adored. I must be adored. They will adore me, and they will love me, and they will honor me, and I will rule them all."

A deep hush descended between us when my mouth closed, a hush thick as velvet.

"That is your greatest dream, your greatest wish," Mariana said, gazing at me, head to the side, smile wide and generous. "Oh, yes, that is your greatest desire. I can feel it within you." She leaned against me, pressed hard against me until I fell back against the chair and surrendered to her. I watched her as she raised her arms over her head, sinuous as a snake, arching back and then forward, diving down to kiss me. She drank deep, deeper still, and, as if from far away or within, I heard the crash of ocean waves against stones, heard them crashing again and again, ceaseless in their passion.

"Tomorrow," said Mariana, taking my hands, placing them upon her warm, warm body, "you will have all you desire. Tomorrow."

The rhythm of the word merged with that of the waves, and I was borne up and away, buffeted by an invisible sea.

The sun was too bright when I woke, and I was angry at having slept so long. "Ready my horse," I told the sorceress, rising, hand to my muzzy head. "I must leave at once."

"You have twilight to wait for, lady knight. It's a few hours still," said Mariana, her back to me as she sat at her spell-working table. I stared while she ground a little of this and a little of that, urging crushed herbs into a bottle as blue as the ocean. "Sup a little. Prepare yourself. This is what you've been waiting for, isn't it? Have patience."

"I am done with patience," I growled, but I sat at the table, anyway, and I ate an apple, and I stared out of the mouth of the cave at the far distant water, agitated, jouncing my leg up and down as if it were possessed by a ghost.

The time crawled by, cruelly slow, as I waited, as I paced, as Mariana worked at her table, sparing no words, no glances for me.

Finally, when the sun began to draw closer to the water, I put on my best armor, and I polished it until it shone brighter than a star. Then I mounted Dana, and I took the blue bottle from the sorceress.

"Will you not kiss me goodbye, your companion these many days?" she asked, gazing up at me through her long dark lashes. I sighed, annoyed, but I leaned down and brushed my lips against her brow.

"There," I told her, and I hastened Dana away, clutching the bottle to my chest.

I did not look back.

At the water's edge this third day, there was no need to summon the muse, for there she was, crawled out half upon the sand, the other half submerged in the water still. She looked like a piece of seaweed left to cook beneath the sun, rumpled and grey-green and dying. But she watched me with bright black eyes as I dismounted Dana from a short distance away; my mare was too nervous to take a step closer to the sea.

I strode down the beach, trying to look impressive even as my armored boots sunk deep into the sand. I had the strangest sensation, as if the shore were not comprised of sand but of little mouths, each of them sucking at my feet, pulling down on my legs; I struggled ferociously with each step. But at last I stood before the muse, blue bottle in hand, and silently mocked her pathetic form bobbing with the ebb and flow of the water.

"It is the third day, hero," she whispered, voice soft, wet. "What have you brought me?"

What *had* I brought her? I stared down at the bottle in my hands, suddenly uncertain. But I was here, and there was only now, and I did not know what to do other than hand her the vessel. The muse stared at me, not the bottle, when she took it from me, claw-like hands curving around the little glass neck as if she would strangle it.

"You want a story, hero," she said then, her voice drawing me in like the sand pulling beneath my boots. "Why should I give you a story?"

I scowled, hands upon my hips. "I know the laws, and I have waited three days. I have summoned you, and you must obey me. Muse, give me the *best* story you have, for with it, I will attain all that I desire."

"All that you desire," she whispered, sinking

deeper into the ocean, never—not once—removing her dark eyes from mine. "Desire," she repeated. The word lingered between us, drifting like flotsam. "Did the sorceress tell you how powerful I am?"

It vexed me that she knew I had spoken with Mariana, that I had used her this many days to coax the muse's favor. I sighed, but I nodded. "Yes, she told me that you were a force of nature and that I must respect you. Though," I laughed a little, "I doubt she has seen you in recent months. You're looking...unwell, O muse." I chuckled to myself, spite rising in the back of my throat as the creature shrank back, stung. Her eyes were wide and wet and dark, muddy, limpid puddles.

"I am worried, in fact," I went on, unmoved, "that you are not up to this task. If your story is not good enough, I shall have to find another muse."

"As if," she whispered softly, "there are so many of us."

"Well, there must be. All the beautiful stories and creations in this world cannot possibly originate from something so hideous, so pathetic as you."

Before my eyes, she grew smaller still, shrinking away from me, shoulders up, chin resting upon her breastbone. "I was..." she began, turning away from me. "I was great once."

"Give me my story," I hissed, waving an arm toward her. "I grow impatient, and I have a long journey back to the castle. Give me my story *now*."

The muse turned her attention to the twinkling bottle in her hands.

"Once," she whispered so softly, I had to lean forward to hear her, "long ago, there was a proud, rich woman who was beautiful and strong and possessed great courage. She had everything a person could wish for. But she was lonely, for she worried that the women who came to love her wanted her for her beauty or her strength or her courage or her riches, never for herself alone. So she set out into the world, dressed as a beggar, seeking a woman who would fall in love with her heart.

"She traveled a long way in her quest, and she met many women, but they were all the same. They thought her beautiful, so they tried to woo her, and the woman's heart grew dark with despair. She dirtied her face, and she tore her clothes, and she finally took to wearing a hooded cloak wherever she went.

"Now none could see her beauty, and when she met women, she conversed with them, telling stories and singing songs. But they fell in love with her pretty voice and her pretty stories. They did not love the woman herself.

"She fell into hopelessness, this woman, and she walked all the way to the sea. 'I would give my soul,' she told the water, 'if someone would love me for my heart alone.' The sea was kind that day, and it listened to her troubles, and water rose up and took from the woman her beauty and her stories and her songs and her body.

"In the great, seething waters, she was rebuilt and reborn, and when the ocean spat her out upon the sand again, she was a repugnant creature, for she had been built from things that, within the water, are lovely to behold, but upon land are ghastly, useless debris. Now she was a creature of the element, and she held all of its stories, for all stories begin in the water. Now she was a muse."

My skin pricked, and I tried to step back, but I found, in that strange moment, that I could not move. I glanced down at my feet, horror-stricken to realize that the sand was sucking me down. When I tried to open my mouth to scream, to rage...I could not speak.

The muse appeared unaware of my discomfort, for she stared down at the bottle in her hands, spellbound, and continued with her tale. "Time passed. The muse watched the world from a distance, submerged beneath the water. Then…amidst the fish and the birds and the fishermen and the children who played upon the shore, she noticed someone.

"A beautiful girl came to the water's edge every day. The beautiful girl came, and she stayed, and she sang to the sea as she plaited her hair, and she laughed at the antics of the fish and the dolphins. She came every day. Every day." The creature's voice had grown hoarse. She paused for a heartbeat.

"The muse watched the girl from the water, watched her laugh at the tumbles the dolphins took, listened to her sing made-up songs to the fish and read aloud from her books of spells and magic. And the muse began to realize something very deep and very true, something that, perhaps, with a simple mortal heart, she might never have known: the muse knew that she loved this girl, but she knew, too, that they could never be together, for she was a monster, and the girl was lovely, but she was also good. And goodness can never love a monster."

I tried again to struggle free of the sand, to speak, to fling myself to the ground, to the water, but I was a statue encased in metal and sand and could do nothing but listen and sink. My anger burned out, replaced by the slithering cold of fear.

"But one day, the muse came upon the sand as the girl was moving down to the edge of the sea. The ocean, again, had mercy in its depths, for what struggled upon the sand was no longer the cobbled-together sea creature, hideous and ill-made, but a woman. A woman and nothing more. Not a beautiful woman, only a woman, naked as she was at the moment of her birth so long ago.

"The girl was no longer a girl now but a woman, too, and she drew near to the muse, spoke with her on the beach. And they came together each day, and they fell in love—this new sorceress and this new muse. They fell in love like no others had before and no others have since. They loved each other fiercely and deeply and truly. They knew love in its purest state, at its heart. And it was…magnificent," the muse whispered. "Wondrous fair."

The sand encompassed my thighs now, the bright silver of my armor flashing back the light of the fading sun as I tried to open my mouth, as I failed.

"But, you see, all things end—where there is a flowing, the ebbing must follow—and the muse's time was up. Her ebb had come, and the ocean pulled her back, and she became again the sea-thing, bonded to the ocean tides." The creature crawled toward me, holding up the bottle. "And the sorceress and the muse despaired, for all they'd ever desired was a shared life, and this love. But they were determined women. They knew they had to build it themselves, if their dream was to be built, and there were spells to undo, and there was great power to summon and daring fortitude to acquire, and when it all came together, when it all," she whispered, eyes alight, "came *together*, hero, they had only one small matter to take care of. Only one."

She came for me, sliding over the sand, one wet green hand in front of the other, as she broke the bottle upon the rock, as the potion began to hiss and smoke, as colors raced across the water, as the sun was eaten up by the sea. The muse moved over the land toward me, mouth wide and open and grinning.

"I will be free," she whispered, "if I devour you. And so I shall, for you are no longer safe, O *Seek*. I know you now. Mariana gave me your name, your greatest dream. She gathered your power for me—bottled your passion, your kisses—and now you are mine."

I had thought her pathetic. Weak. Worthless. But as she leered, as her mouth grew, as the blackness spiraled out to meet me, I knew the truth: that she was a force and an element, and I had been wrong about everything.

There was a long, dull moment of waves and birds heckling. Sounds and sensations, the coolness of water, the pressure of sand and surf.

The woman opened her eyes, struggling on heavy, wobbly legs, staring down at her chainmaille-clad hands, blinking. She tore the metal gloves off, and then she pulled her feet out of the boots, leaving the things encased in the sand as she stumbled up and out of the pull of the tide. Off came the breastplate, and off came the rest of the armor, and she left it all where it fell, discarded silver upon the shore.

"Whoa, whoa," she murmured to the mare. Dana, was it? The horse flared her nostrils at this woman who looked so like that woman, her woman. But it was not her woman. It was not, and the horse did not understand it, but she knew it, too, and she sidestepped the outstretched hands, rearing up, turning and racing, kicking up her heels over the beach and through the meadow and into the wood.

The woman watched her go, laughing a little, giddy, heady. She set off in bare feet then, down the path she had never walked but knew so well, knew by heart, the path that led to the cave along the cliffs.

The sorceress stood in the mouth of the cave, watching, waiting. And when the woman came around the curve in the path, Mariana stood on tiptoes, hands on hips, biting her lip and scarcely able to breathe.

But the woman, the muse, the creature, ran the rest of the way, swept Mariana up, brought her down to kiss someone else's lips, but now her lips, the muse's lips, and she kissed her again and again and again until they were laughing and weeping and entwined together, limbs akimbo. Again and again, they embraced, and Mariana sank down to the floor of the cave, skirts mounded around her, head in her hands as she wept, the lonely years running down into the earth as the muse crouched down beside her, ancient as tide and salt, whispering into her hair, her ear, pressing lips there, and there again, telling her the truth, that it was finally all right, that it had happened. It had finally happened. They were together again, together for always. Forever.

And the beautiful Lady Ella married a fair-haired peasant girl who had completed none of the tasks set forth by stern King Raul but had fallen in love with the princess for her irreverent sense of humor and her compassionate heart.

Down, down, at the bottom of the ocean, a new creature lurks. She is hideous, and she is angry, but after soaking for years in the embrace of never-changing tides, she will rise up to the line of the shore, destined to devour. As all muses must.

OUR LADY OF WOLVES

I'm afraid of the church. It's broken, falling apart; from the inside, the walls lean ominously toward me. The rafters sag. The windows—once spangled with colored glass—lay broken at my bare feet, and I have to pick my way carefully. There's a flutter of pigeons overhead, their startled voices admonishing me: *How dare you come here? This is no place for the likes of you.*

My heart thunders, pounding in my throat and along my fingers, under the lines of my palms. I'm slick with sweat. The heat hovers, but truly I'm hot with fear, with prickling awareness. Every sound makes me shudder, makes me scurry to find out where, or what, it's coming from.

The church was overtaken by the forest long ago. It holds the quiet of the trees and the scuttling sounds of a thousand little lives, a thousand tiny heartbeats. I still myself, or try to, when I jump again at a pigeon's wings flapping.

I've come this far. I can't lose my nerve now.

The statue is at the back of the church, covered in dark moss, cracked and crumbling. But her face stares at me beatifically as I make my cautious way down the center aisle, drawing ever closer. She wears a grey mantle over her head, and at the heart of her expression is a soft smile, a kind smile. But her serenity contrasts starkly with the massive carved wolf pressed against her stone legs, gazing out with narrowed eyes, hungry mouth hanging open.

I take a deep breath.

This is what I came for. To plead with Our Lady of Wolves.

"Look," I say nervously, flinching as twenty pigeons take off from their roost overhead at the sound of my voice. I'm shaking, but I kneel down before the statue, mindful to place my bare knees on either side of a sharp slice of glass. The pebbled floor digs into my skin.

I fold my hands as my grandmother used to do every morning, when she spoke the prayer aloud. She was the last one I knew who believed in Our Lady of Wolves. Now my mother scoffs whenever I mention the Lady, refuses to talk about her at all. And the villagers turned their backs on her, and this church, decades ago.

"Look," I begin again, clearing my throat. "I'm sorry that…" I bite my lip. What, truly, can I say? How can I excuse our negligence? It has been years since anyone came to this church in earnest, and that isn't my fault, and I am the one who is here now, but I feel a pressing need to apologize for my village. "I'm sorry that no one's come for so long," I whisper to the statue, as sweat glides in a single, salty line down my back, craving an itch. I ignore it. "I don't know if you remember my grandmother, Adele." My voice is steadier, louder now. "She loved you so much. I've never stopped thinking about you, no matter what everyone says," I add quickly. "And now that this is happening, now that…" I stare at my hands in my lap. "I remember the stories my grandmother told me, how you helped and comforted people in hard times."

I sigh and make fists, nails digging into my palms, because I'm crying, hiccupping, sobbing, and I can't stop, but I have to stay sharp, aware. Crying doesn't help; crying is for the weak, and I've survived this long. I am not *weak*.

"We're in trouble," I whisper, glancing up at the statue. Unmoving, she seems to peer down, curving toward me, eyes steady. I breathe out. "We're going to die. All of us. There aren't many of us left now and... We need your help. And I'm sorry to ask. I'm sorry to ask this after what everyone let happen to the church, to you..." I trail off, staring forlornly at the places where chunks of stone are missing from her base, her dress. One edge of her face is missing, too, chiseled away or broken, but she still looks beautiful.

"Please help us, Lady," I whisper, as the sun slips down to touch the earth and the trees murmur in the slight wind—then stop.

The riot of wings in the rafters above my head stills; the pigeons are silent.

All around me, the world is hushed, made mute.

I hold my breath.

No.

No. It's impossible. There is always time between attacks. *Always.* I'd carefully timed it, made certain to set off into the forest at high noon, on the heels of the last attack—three killed last night—because I'm not *stupid.* I took every precaution, planned it all out.

Dread settles in the pit of my stomach, heavy as a stone.

I shoot to my feet, cutting my shin on the shard of glass; a warm wet trickle of blood slides down my leg to stain the pebbles. I need to run or climb or do *something*, but I'm frozen, heart thundering, eyes wide, as the darkness enters the church. There's scrabbling outside the sanctuary walls.

I'm going to die.

Every part of my body aches to run, to move, but there's no place for me to go, so I do the simplest thing: I step backward, and I feel the sharp-edged piece of glass beneath my foot, feel it slice, and stifle a cry. Still, I press back, push my shoulder blades hard against the statue, and it isn't comfort that it gives me but solidity, something certain.

I hear them, then—close by.

Their scales make a *shushing* sound over the stones. There are many of them, so many, because the murmur of their movement grows louder as more and more of them crawl through the doorway, into the sanctuary.

I cry out now—there's no sense in keeping quiet—and I stare in horror at the shadows bobbing along the floor, becoming thicker, darker, creeping closer, and I just want it to be quick, but they are *never* quick: the sharpness of their mouths pricks you and tears you and savors you as you scream and scream, as my sister screamed and screamed…

Silence.

I gasp.

A thin, bare moment passes, and I look about me, gape at the light that's returned, but I'm trembling so deeply that my legs collapse. I'm almost relieved to fall down to the hard stone floor. My head dashes against the pebbles, and for a moment, my vision goes all white.

I lie motionless.

What…happened?

I don't understand.

They were here, and now they're gone.

They would never have journeyed so far on the hunt and then turned back unsatisfied, prey abandoned. They never leave prey alive. Their hunger is too deep.

But somehow I'm alone. They left me alone. Alive.

Alive.

I gather the last scraps of courage I possess and crawl carefully over the glass and stones to the edge of the door and peer out, heart racing.

Green. Green and sunlight, and the path out to the forest is empty, bright, clear.

They're really gone.

"Oh, gods." I put a hand to my neck, feel the damp stick of sweat beneath my fingers. I'm alive. Impossibly, like a dream, I'm alive.

But how?

My mind can't make sense of it; my head hurts too much to think. And then... Then I just know.

"You." I turn in awe, swallow the lump in my throat, and lower myself until my forehead is pressed flat against the stone floor. I sob, sob so hard I fear my ribs will crack. "You did this," I whisper to the statue at the back of the sanctuary. "You saved me." I tilt up my head, gaze at her smooth, lovely face, and I exhale a breath I didn't realize I'd been holding. "Please," I whisper. I'm afraid to ask, afraid that nothing will happen, but I'm afraid not to ask, because what if... What if there's still hope?

"Please save us," I choke out around my tears. "Please save us all. Please...come."

Her broken face smiles down upon me, indulgent, serene. Silent.

"It happened," I tell her hotly, running my hands through my hair, tugging at the long braid in frustration. "I'm telling you, it *happened*."

"Kelly, the heat's gotten to you." My mother sighs

as her shaking hands bend the vine through another tiny opening, tightening the base of the basket. "I can't believe you went there, so near to the forest," she says for, perhaps, the hundredth time. "You could have been killed, and then—"

"And then?" I splutter, hands spread. "And then *what*, Mother? We're *all* going to die, sooner rather than later, and you're not *listening*. The Lady saved me. It happened. They were coming for me and…" I gulp down the memory, glance away. "I was going to die. But they stopped, and they went back, and they disappeared, and that has *never* happened before. You know it!"

She pauses in her weaving, looks at me, really looks. Her mouth curves down, but—for a heartbeat—that same spark that she used to have, the one I miss so much, comes back to life in her eyes, and she wonders, head cocked.

But just as quickly, it's gone, and her eyes fall dark.

"Mother," I plead, "it's just as Grandmother said… I prayed to the Lady, and she came in my time of need—"

"Your grandmother was a zealous woman with strange, morbid notions—"

"She saved me." I stare at my mother, desperate to make her understand. "Our Lady saved me from them."

"No, Kelly." She cradles her head in her hands. "No one gets that kind of reprieve," she says softly, gently. "I know your sister's death was harder on you. Perhaps that's why you've imagined—"

"*Imagined*," I whisper, shaking my head.

My mother stares at me, eyes sad, and I rise. I cross to her, and I kiss her cheek, her thin-as-paper cheek, and I leave the house, taking the stairs two at a time, because I love her, and she loves me, but in this, she will never believe me, and I should have known better than to think she might.

It's not dark, not yet. But night will fall soon, so everyone is shutting up their houses, sealing them tight. There are only two other people out on the streets beside myself, and they're hurrying, heads down, hastening home before the sky goes black.

You don't stay out after dark, and you don't come out until late morning, and even then, sometimes the attacks are irregular. We try to find patterns, but they're always defying them. We can't predict when or where the next attacks will occur, and all we *can* count on is the fact that they could creep in at *any* time and take you away, eat you up, and that's just the way of things now, isn't it? That's what Mother says.

There are thirty people left in a village that used to boast hundreds. That's not *the way* of things. That's tragic. But we can't leave. We'd have to venture into the forest that surrounds town on all sides to leave, and everyone knows that that's where they live, where they skulk.

People have tried to escape. Of course they've tried.

And we have all heard them screaming.

I rub at my eyes as I walk, aimless. It's not my mother's fault that she doesn't believe me. I'd be hard pressed to believe the tale myself if I hadn't lived it. Everybody knows that once they begin to hunt, they're unstoppable, single-minded.

I shudder, duck into the doorway of an abandoned house—there are more abandoned houses than lived-in ones now—and watch the sun between the far-off trees, tilting ever closer to the edge of the earth. I should go back. I have to get indoors, but I'm frustrated and in no mood for my mother's placating. I chew on my lip, thinking.

Edward had a house on the outskirts of town,

before he was…caught. It's empty now. No one moved in, of course; it's too close to the forest, and all of the remaining townsfolk are clustered together in a scattering of houses in the middle of the village. It's safer that way, or everyone says it's safer that way.

But the things haven't figured out locks yet, and I've always felt safe enough in Edward's old house myself. Sometimes I go there during the day to be alone, to think, though I've never passed a night there. But after today… For the first time in my life, I feel brave. Or reckless. Maybe a little bit of both.

I've spent nights in other vacant houses around town, nearer houses. Mother knows I like to get away. She won't worry—not any more than usual.

"Our Lady of Wolves," I whisper, as I start moving, hurrying along the dusky streets. There are no more people in sight. That's a bad sign. My heart somersaults in my chest as I trot, then run, then madly race and trip toward Edward's house, its dark window eyes peering down at me, curtainless.

"Our Lady of Wolves," I whisper again, when I'm safe inside, when I've shut and locked the door, checked every window, checked every door, swallowed the knot of fear lodged in my throat. "Our Lady of Wolves, who is the Mother. Sacred is thy name. Stand before the darkness, stand before the descent. Lead me past the shadows, to the land of eternal peace, your wolves my guides…" I frown and try to remember the rest—I must have heard my grandmother repeat the prayer a thousand times—but the lines are lost to me now. I shrug and whisper, "Amen."

Then I sigh, leaning against the hallway wall. *Your wolves my guides.* That part kind of makes me fret, because the wolves are dead. All of the wolves were killed, *eaten,* decades ago. There's nothing bigger than a squirrel out there in the woods now, and hardly any squirrels, because *they* are ravenous.   Which is why they've come to town. Which is why they've come for us.

I creep around the house, over every floor of every room, inspecting all of the nooks for monsters, and then, finding none, I drag the couch in front of the entryway door, and I drag the kitchen table in front of the back door, and I slide a bookcase in front of the largest window. And I go upstairs, into the big bedroom, and push the heavy bed up against the bolted door.

Hauling the coverings off of the bed, I make a little nest of the comforter and sheets and curl up in the center of the floor, and I try to go to sleep. I close my eyes, will my muscles to relax. They don't. Can't. Because I know they're coming, and every part of my body is on edge. The tiny hairs along the back of my neck stand on end. I'm strung so tightly that when I sigh, I shiver.

I hear them.

I sigh again, just a little, breathing out. I hear them outside, their bodies brushing loud against the dry grass as they creep. They're early tonight. The sun hasn't set all the way. I pull the comforter over my head and try to stop up my ears, but I can still hear them.

I don't know if they think. They hunt, but is hunting just instinct? Nothing more than an insatiable hunger? If they do think, I believe that they like their own sound, the way it drives the fear, like a rusty nail, deeper and deeper into the hearts of their prey.

I close my eyes and find myself praying again: *Our Lady of Wolves, who is the Mother*...

At the bedroom door comes a knock.

I sit bolt upright, the blanket falling away from me.

I was alone. I checked the house from its topmost floor all the way down to the basement, checked every cupboard, looked under all the tables. I was alone, and not a single *soul* goes out after dark. People never leave their houses after *they* prowl out of the woods.

It's not possible. It's as impossible as the things turning away from a hunt—no, *more* impossible, because that happened... That happened because Our Lady of Wolves—

The knock comes again.

I flatten myself upon the floor and peer under the bed propped up against the door, squint to see under the door itself.

There are boots.

I don't even think. I rise, almost stumbling, and push away the bed with strength I don't have, fumbling with shaking hands at the bolt, and then I open the door wide.

And I stare, open-mouthed.

A woman. There's a woman with hair short-shorn and ragged over her ears and eyes, eyes that follow mine in the gloom. The first things I notice besides her dark piercing gaze are her clothes; they're odd. She's dressed...not like us, not like the people from town with our simple lightweight garments. She's wearing heavy, ragged layers, and a hood hangs back from her shoulders.

I'm staring.

But I'm not staring because of her unusual clothes or even because she's a stranger in a village that hasn't seen a stranger in over thirty years.

I'm staring because of the wolf at her feet.

It *is* a wolf. It has to be. It stares at me with golden-brown eyes, mouth open a little in a pant, long tongue dangling from an equally long snout. Its great brush of a tail wags back and forth, back and forth.

"Who...what..." I whisper, and she starts to speak, but I hiss, "Wait," because it's ingrained in me, because I can't forget to be afraid, and I reach forward, grabbing her arm. I drag her into the bedroom, and the wolf lopes in, too, and I shut the door behind us, bolt it, breathing hard.

They've never gotten inside before, but it's a strange night, and I always feel safer with as many doors as possible between me and them.

I'm facing the woman, and she's gazing at me; the wolf, again, is poised at her feet.

"Who are you?" I gasp in the dim room. I don't dare strike one of the matches on the dresser, light the little candle there. No one in the village uses candles anymore. Light draws them near. Or, at least, we think it does.

"How did you find us?" I persist, breathless. "Did you walk through the forest? Where have you come from? What...I..." I shake my head and swallow the rest of my words, too overcome with emotion to speak. I open my hands to her, palms up, waiting.

She stares at me quizzically.

I think she's my age. Maybe. Over twenty, below thirty. It's impossible to tell for certain. Her eyes are fast; she notices everything. Her lips remain closed in a curving, unyielding line. She spares a glance for the wolf seated beside her as he draws his tongue back into his toothy mouth.

"Who are *you*?" she asks then, her voice soft, light.

I start a little, run my hand through my hair, along my braid. "Kelly," I say, and before I can feel stupid about it, I ask her the most important question: "Did Our Lady of Wolves send you?"

She holds my gaze for another long moment, but then she shakes her head, lips turning up into a subtle smile. "No. No one sent me."

"Oh. Because..." I swallow and point to the wolf, now lying with its large paws stretched out. "You have a wolf! I went to the church today, and I prayed for help, so I thought...."

Her eyes study my face, my features, while her own expression remains calm and unreadable. It's unnerving, having this stranger gaze at me so intensely.

She says nothing.

My illusions are crumbling, but I cling desperately to their foundation. "How...how did you get here? How did you travel through the woods?"

She sits down on the bed, leans back, long black-clad legs dangling over the side of the stripped mattress. The wolf leaps up beside her in one effortless thrust and flops over, its shoulder pressing against her hip.

"I got here on my legs," she says easily then, dark eyes twinkling.

I stare at her, stricken speechless. She's joking? There are monsters stalking us outside, and she's evading my questions with a joke?

I shake my head in disbelief. "No one has come to our village in over thirty years. We've been living on canned food and some shriveled crops and...and mostly *squirrels*. But the squirrels are dying now. We are dying. Every day we are *dying*, because *they* are getting stronger, and we're getting weaker and fewer, and I went to the church of Our Lady of Wolves today, and I prayed for her help, and you're telling me that this is *coincidence*? That you braved the infested woods and showed up on the very same day that I prayed for help, when no one else has *ever* come?"

She challenges my hot gaze with her cool, steady one. "Whatever you choose to believe or not believe is of no consequence to me. I'm a traveler—"

"A traveler?" I gape. "There are no travelers. How could you travel *anywhere* when they are *everywhere*?"

She raises her chin then, one eyebrow lifted in an imperious curve. "They fear me."

I fall back, as if I were shoved. "Fear you?" I

whisper, scrabbling to make sense of the notion. "But…why?"

She sighs, glancing away.

"Please," I whisper then, and I don't even care—I don't—because I'm on my knees before this stranger now, this stranger whose name I don't know, who won't tell me where she's come from or how she got here, and I press my hands against her knees, stare up at her with tear-filled eyes. "Please help us," I plead, voice cracking. "We're dying. If they're afraid of you, if you can destroy them, then we…"

She shakes her head quickly and shifts, as if she's been made uncomfortable by my closeness, by my begging. "You misunderstand. It's not so simple," she mutters, but I shake my head, too, clasping my hands together upon her lap now as tears trace down my cheeks.

"Tell me, then. Tell me how to make them fear *me*. Please tell me how to stop them," I sob beneath her dark, even gaze.

And in that moment, her face changes, softens, smoothes, as she leans forward, as she reaches out with her gloved hand to wipe away one of my tears.

I breathe out. It's an unfamiliar gesture, an intimate gesture. People don't touch one another often here. It's easier if we don't get too close.

She exhales heavily. "No one's come to this village for thirty years," she murmurs, as if suddenly understanding, as if turning the thought over in her head.

I realize then that I'm still kneeling, still leaning against her with my hands on her knees, and her hand has not left my cheek. Her fingers linger, tracing the contours of my cheekbone, my jaw. I tremble and close my eyes.

"We're dying," I whisper, repeating a phrase I've used far too often throughout my life. "We can't stop them ourselves. We've tried, and too many have lost their lives. Please…help us."

I open my eyes, try to snare her gaze, but her head is down as she rises, as I lean away from her. Then she's helping me up, enveloping my fingers with her strong hands, lifting me easily to my feet.

We're standing close, much too close, and when I look up at her, I can't help but shiver as a darkness descends behind her eyes, and this woman, this stranger says, "I cannot save you."

My legs wobble, and my heart seizes as hope struggles to survive within me, but I refuse to look away. "What is your name?" I ask her, dauntless.

"Triste," she replies, eyebrow raised.

"Well, Triste," I say evenly, "like I told you before, I prayed to Our Lady of Wolves for help, and then you arrived. That has to mean something. Doesn't it mean something?" I search her gaze, but there is no flicker of acknowledgment in her eyes. Still, I won't give up. I *can't* give up. "I'm…I'm begging you to help us. Just tell me—why do they fear you?"

My jaw clenches as I await her reply. I have imagined them in torment, suffering, dying a hundred times. But the reality of it seems impossible, like a story, a *lie*. How could they fear anyone, anything? Fire does not burn them; weapons do not cut them. They are invincible.

"I take their lives," she says simply.

"Take their…lives," I whisper, and I feel myself pale. "How is it possible to kill them—"

She turns away from me, but I press on.

"Their *teeth*! How *fast* they are. So many people have *tried* to kill them and failed—"

"They weren't meant to kill them. That's why they failed."

"But you are—"

"No. I'm not meant to kill them, either. Not here. Not now."

I stare. She sighs.

110

It's fully dark, but the moon is bright, and I can still make out her lithe form, her eyes, wet and wide. My throat is so dry, I cough into my fist and then crouch down, rest my head on my knees.

"It's over, then," I whisper.

I had truly hoped…had half-believed…

I feel her kneel beside me, hear her sigh again.

"Triste," I tell her, words muffled but sharp and edged with tears, "everyone I have ever known is dead now, or destined to die. Last night, three more people were killed. *Three*. We used to have thirty-three people here. We used to have hundreds." My voice catches, but I swallow and shake my head against my knees. "I watched my sister get ripped apart by them. I *saw* it happen. And I couldn't do anything, *nothing,* to stop them. I'll never forget how she…" My whole body trembles. But I can't think about that, about her. I have to stay here and now. "And then at the church today, they were coming for me. They were *coming,* but they *stopped*. It was a miracle. Or I thought it was."

"They *almost* got you today," she says softly, and I raise my head, nodding, but I don't look at her.

"They almost got me last week, too, so…" I swipe an arm over my wet face and stand up, sniffling. Triste stands up beside me. "Sooner or later, I'll die. We'll all die. And," I sigh, laughing darkly, "that's just the way things are."

The brittle words sharpen the air between us.

Exhausted and hopeless, I gaze at Triste's moonlit outline. Her short hair stands up at odd angles, and she runs her hands through it now, just like I do whenever I'm nervous. I wonder if she's nervous.

"What do you want?" she asks me; her voice is piercing.

"Help us," I tell her, without a breath or a thought or a heartbeat between the words. "We need your help."

She sighs and sits back down on the edge of the bed. Her wolf sleeps against the headboard, and Triste's hand reaches out to lazily stroke its fur. Long, awkward moments stretch between us.

I clasp my hands before me, holding my breath.

Then she speaks the words I've longed to hear: "I'll try to help you."

I gasp, startled. "You…You will?"

"Come with me when I leave," she murmurs. "All of you. And…" She spreads her hands. "I will do my best to spare you pain."

Did I fall asleep? Am I dreaming this?

I stand, move to her in the dark, sit next to her on the bed. And then I put out my hands, my arms, and I twine them around her, embrace her, drawing her against me.

"*Thank* you," I whisper, breathing easily, without aching, for the first time today. For the first time in years.

This close, Triste smells of ash, of wood smoke and wind. She's tense in my arms, but then her face turns toward me in the dark, and I feel her breath against my neck.

I shiver.

"Triste," I say, and my lips are so dry, I lick them.

She murmurs against my neck: "Yes." And I can feel her; she's moving, trembling against me.

And then the light shifts, or the room tilts, or maybe something within me just wakes up, becomes what it was always meant to be, because, all of the sudden, the whole world feels different—alive, *real*. It feels like velvet upon my skin.

I bow my head nearer to Triste's bare neck.

Before my sister died—before they tore her apart—she had a boyfriend. Cassie was one of very few unmarried young women left in our village. James was eligible and just about her age… And those, I thought, were terrible reasons to decide to fall in love with each other—scarcity, age compatibility—but Cassie was an optimist; she always tried to make the best of things.

And he did make her happy. So happy she forgot to do the simplest, most ingrained tasks, like locking the doors at night and always keeping one eye fastened to the sun.

Once, I found them tangled together on an old couch in an abandoned house on the outskirts of town…and I left, cheeks hot, without making my presence known.

I do think she loved him. And he loved her. *They* took him, tore him apart, too, not one week after I watched her die. Some of the villagers say he gave himself to them willingly, even sought them out, because his heart was so broken.

I've never had feelings like that for anyone. All of our young people are gone, dead, and everyone else is spoken for or depressed or too preoccupied with survival to spare a thought for romance. Villagers teased Cassie and James about it, about how silly they were being, kissing each other right in the town square while monsters prowled and neighbors died. But, really, everyone was happy for them, happy to know that something *normal* was going on in the village. It gave them hope.

But just because there is no one here for me never stopped me from daydreaming about the possibility. About what it might have been like had there been a woman right next door who made me blush, just like James made Cassie blush. A woman who made me forget to be safe. I'd imagined it lots of times, mostly at night, when my mother was asleep and couldn't hear my sobs.

But I haven't thought about that in a very long time.

When Triste turns to me in the dark, when her warm, sweet breath tickles my neck, a shock lances through me, and I wonder if my body will ever stop trembling. And I realize, in that moment, that I don't want it to.

"Do you…" I swallow. What can I say? I have no words, and it's awkward, how I angle toward her mouth, how I brush my lips against hers, less like a kiss than a question. *Do you want to? Thank you. Do you want to?* I can't think of how else to ask it, but her mouth opens beneath mine, and then we're kissing on the edge of the bed, my arms still wrapped about her. Very carefully, very softly, she places her hand against the curve of my thigh.

Our savior, touching me.

"Down, Star," she growls, and I don't understand what she means, not until the wolf shifts and leaps politely off of the bed. I laugh a little, embarrassed, but she presses me down gently against the mattress, and then she's kissing me again, pulling off her gloves, divesting herself of her cloak and then one, two, three of her shirts, and she's helping me out of mine, and the cool lick of air against my bare chest makes me shiver again, but I'm too far gone: I only feel the hiss of her skin against my skin, the sting of it, the strange taste of body against body, wonders I've never known before, so delicious. I vow to savor them all.

But I'm awkward. Of course I'm awkward. I hit my jaw on her shoulder when I tilt back my head, moaning, and she laughs a little when she dives in for a feral kiss and our teeth click together. I'm red, flushed, blushing terribly, but her fingers trace over my breasts, over the curve of bared hips revealed when I shove off my skirt, and then…and then, she's cupping the rise of my behind, and she's sliding down, and she's between my legs, and my shins wrap around her as if they've known how to do this, have been waiting to do this, always.

She feels familiar. In my imaginings, thought and

re-thought a hundred times, a thousand, the woman who made my heart race had a face I could not quite see, save for the hint of a shadowy smile. It wasn't really her, wasn't Triste, that woman in my daydreams, but I know Triste all the same. Know her hot, slippery skin, her breath so loud in the stillness, and my breath, too…

It's almost like a dance.

I feel new as she touches me, as her fingers seek, warm and wanting, as her mouth devours mine, and I *don't* feel any of the old guilt, the fear, the misery. I feel nothing but *good* as she touches and tastes and teases, and I breathe out a whimper, a shuddering sigh as she lifts up my hips, her own pushed between my legs, pressing down in an undulating rhythm that suddenly turns urgent.

As she touches me, fingers tracing patterns between my breasts, down and over my ribs, around the pool of my stomach…I don't think about *them.* I think of nothing at all.

I think nothing, but I feel everything, and I see a thousand starbursts of light, of color, behind my eyes. There's the brush of dry, dirty mattress under my back and beneath the balls of my feet as I press up and against her. I crave the heat, the warmth of her body, and my body is burning, all of me, burning, and when her soft, warm mouth claims my own again, I moan, and she devours that, too, that guttural syllable of need.

In the dark, we move together like nocturnal things; we have no need of light.

My eyes are slits against the sun.

I breathe out, clear my throat, sit up.

I'm on the mattress in Edward's house, my clothes discarded upon the floor. Naked, I slide to the edge of the bed and stand, heart hammering within me, because I'm alone. No Triste, no wolf.

They're gone. Both of them, gone.

I can't believe it.

I throw my clothes on, buttoning and lacing with shaking hands, and stuff my feet into my shoes. Then I listen carefully at the crack of the closed door, because no matter what's happened, I'm not *stupid*, and when I don't hear the slither of scales upon the floorboards, when I don't hear anything, I unbolt the lock and swing the door open wide.

She's not in the hallway. She's not downstairs. She's not in the house. She's not on the front or back lawn, and as I stand in the tall grass behind the house, fingers curled into fists, I feel small parts of myself breaking, shattering, sharding away from my body. She's gone, just like that. And I can't believe it. But it's the truth.

She disappeared as impossibly as she came.

Trembling fingers graze the raw skin of my neck where, last night, she pressed her lips. My mouth is sore, swollen from her kisses. She wasn't a daydream. She was here; my body is testament to that.

I slept with her. A stranger, a savior. I slept with the savior, but she was no savior, because she left.

I feel so empty.

I turn and walk away from Edward's old house; I'll never come back here, not ever again—not for as long as I survive. An impossible thing happened here, a lovely thing, a dream, and I will forever be too tired to remember it.

But as I think these thoughts and tread along Main Street, there's a pricking at the back of my neck, and I pause, listening.

Voices. Many voices.

I round the bend, and there, just beyond the emptied-out grocery store, are all of the villagers, everyone who's left: my mother and twenty-eight others. The last survivors.

And Triste.

She stands amongst the people, my people, her dark, short-cropped head tilted to the side, listening to Albert as he gestures wildly at her and widens his milky eyes. I see Annie and Levvy standing side by side, listening to Albert, too, but my mother stares at Triste, only at Triste, her thin mouth closed in a firm line.

Star, the wolf, panting at Triste's feet, notices me first, and then Triste turns her head, parts her lips, drinks me in with her eyes, wide and dark, and my heart pounds in the stillness of late morning.

I breathe out.

She's here. She did not leave us, did not go; she kept her promise. She's *keeping* her promise. She's *here*.

"If you'll excuse me," Triste says then, and she moves past Albert, past my mother, through the surly, muttering crowd, and walks toward me, her face cool and expressionless save for the tiny curve at the corner of her mouth, a sly smile meant for me alone. Her eyes gleam black and deep, and when she steps close, my body aches in all the right places.

"I've tried," she says softly, sighing. "They won't listen to me. They don't believe that safety lies beyond the woods, that I could guide them there."

I sigh, too, and shake my head. "You have to understand... All we know of the woods is that people die there, that...*they* live there," I tell her. "The forest, to us, promises only death."

A flicker of sorrow darkens her features. She breathes in deeply through her nose and, for a moment, closes her eyes. "But even death would be better than this scrabbling existence," she murmurs, pressing a hand to her forehead. "Wouldn't it?" The sudden intensity of her gaze startles me. I open my mouth but say nothing. "You're surrounded by them, trapped. They kill your people, *eat* your people…" She blinks, turns away, and a shiver races through me; my arms prickle with goosebumps.

"This is how we live, Triste," I tell her, voice little more than a whisper. "It's all we know how to do. We don't take risks. We barely dare to hope. We just…survive."

"There's a better way, a better place," she says, eyes soft but watchful. "You asked me to take you there, and I can. I will," she breathes out, straightening, "if you can convince them to come." She gestures toward the assembled villagers; they glare at us with suspicious eyes, arms crossed, fists tight.

I quake beneath my mother's shrewd gaze.

But this is it. This is the moment I've been waiting for; this is *our chance* at a new life, a *real* life, somewhere else. And freedom. I believe that Triste can save us.

I stiffen and stride into the heart of the mob.

"We have to go," I tell them simply, without preamble.

Twenty-nine pairs of eyes flick toward Triste, who has pulled up her hood; her eyes are no longer visible beneath the black curve of fabric.

"Mother," I say then, going to her, reaching for her hands and shaking my head. She holds my fingers but eyes me cagily. "We all have to go. Now," I insist. "I told you what happened yesterday. I told you—"

"Kelly…" she sighs.

But I am determined. I turn toward the others. "I went to the church yesterday. I spoke to Our Lady of Wolves!" I shout, and the villagers glance to one another, murmuring behind their hands. I feel their eyes and straighten my shoulders. "I was about to be torn apart— they came for me—but I prayed to Our Lady, I begged her to come and help us, and they turned back! They left! I believe," I say, softly now, because everyone has fallen silent, "that Our Lady of Wolves sent Triste to help us."

"Oh, Kelly," my mother moans, voice tight.

"Listen to me." I clench my jaw. "We're all going to die if we don't go with her."

"We're going to die if we *go* with her, Kelly," says my mother, and I turn to her, exasperation flaring along my bones. I sigh and sputter and start to argue, but Triste rests a hand upon my shoulder, and I turn to face her.

"I'm leaving at noon," she says, pointing up to the sun as it crawls closer to the center of the sky. "I hope that you will all choose to go through the forest with me." Her voice is gentle, patient, coaxing. Her hand slides down my arm to clasp briefly at my hand, and then she turns and strides away, long, easy steps, aiming toward the edge of town, in the opposite direction of Edward's old house.

I stand, torn, watching Star and Triste grow small in the distance, curling and uncurling my hands as I gaze from face to face…and there are so few faces, so many fewer than there were this time last week, this time a month ago.

My heart hurts.

"Kelly," says my mother, and her hand presses against my sleeve. I look at her, ache at the sight of tears standing in her eyes. "Kelly…" She breathes out, shakes her head. "Our Lady of Wolves isn't—"

"She sent Triste to *help* us," I whisper, and I'm grasping my mother's shoulders, fingers curved around them, holding them tightly. She feels so thin, so small. "Triste will help us. We'll escape. We'll leave this place. We'll be *safe*," I tell her, but my mother won't stop shaking her head, won't stop crying, and I realize my cheeks are damp; I'm crying, too.

"Kelly—"

"Mother, please," I moan, throwing my arms

around her neck, pressing my face against her shoulder just as I used to do when I was a little girl. "I want you to be *safe*. I don't want you to be afraid anymore. I don't want any of us to be afraid. And this is the *only way*."

I feel her exhale a heavy breath. She draws back, takes my hands, gazes hard into my eyes. I stare at her, weeping, and watch her expression change again and again—stubbornness, sorrow, affection, resignation...

"What's done is done," she says finally, letting my hands fall with a gentle pat and turning to face the others. "Kelly is right. It's time for us to move on. Let us go."

Voices rise up, a tangle of words and sobs, but by the time the sun takes its place at the top of the sky, we have joined Triste where she waits at the edge of the forest—all thirty of us, the last of us, standing together.

Triste, Star on her heels, comes to stand beside me, and she slips her hand into mine, gazes down at me solemnly. My mother's eyes widen as she glances from me to Triste and back to me again. I smile softly and reach for her hand, too, and we walk with the others, unwavering, into the woods.

I feel so strange.

Is it too hot? No, that's not it. I think it's the air... Something's wrong with the air, or—

We move beneath the trees, and Triste squeezes my hand, but then, oddly, I shake my head and blink my eyes, because I see the villagers, my mother, as if from far away, as if they're far below and I'm floating above them, but that's not right, because I'm holding my mother's hand—

"Hurry, Kelly," Triste says softly, kindly. "Before they come."

I walk faster. We're deep in the forest now, and I'm not afraid; I'm light, free. We've left the village; we've left it all back there, all of the bad memories laid to rest.

Then I hear *them* moving behind us.

"No... They're coming," I whisper to Triste, but she just shakes her head, squeezes my hand again.

"It's all right," she tells me.

All right? No, something's wrong...isn't it? Something *is* wrong, because I hear screaming all of the sudden, but— I glance around me, behind me, count, and everyone's here. We're all here, walking together, but still I hear screaming and tearing, and I breathe out.

There's a clearing up ahead, between the trees, but it looks strangely dark, like the doorway to a darkened room. My mother lets go of my hand, and Triste and I stand aside as the villagers pass us by, as, heads down, they enter the clearing. I think it's a clearing. My mother is the last to remain, besides Triste and me, and she glances at us sidelong, silent, eyes bright with tears, before she steps forward, through and into the darkness.

"Are you ready?" asks Triste, and when I gaze up into her deep, black eyes, I feel for the first time in my life the surety of peace.

"Will you tell me something first?"

She inclines her head, places a hand against my cheek.

"Why did you come? Why did you knock on the bedroom door at Edward's house? How did you know—"

"I came," she says, smiling beatifically and bending down to press a sweet, lingering kiss against my lips, "because you asked me to."

"Oh," I breathe, eyes hot, stinging, streaming with tears. "Oh," I say again, thinking of the church, of the statue and the wolf and my grandmother, my grandmother who prayed fervently to Our Lady as she lay on her bed, as she took her last breath...

And I forget to be afraid, and I *know* peace when I enter the darkness, because my grandmother's prayer—the whole prayer—comes back to me. It surrounds me, as if it's being spoken by a thousand, a million voices, whispering together. I sigh and nod and squeeze Triste's hand back as we pass into the clearing together.

Our Lady of Wolves, who is the Mother,
sacred is thy name.
Stand before the darkness,
stand before the descent.
Lead me past the shadows
to the land of eternal peace,
your wolves my guides.
Mother of Death, Lady of Reaping,
be with me now in the hour of my death.

Amen.

WE GROW ACCUSTOMED TO THE DARK

The Rapture happens on a Tuesday, on the way home from school. I'm walking arm in arm with Celia, because screw the other kids; she's my girlfriend, and they can go fuck themselves if they don't like it (and they don't, but whatever). I'm so sick of always looking around, checking to see who's watching before kissing my girlfriend's nose or holding her hand, and, I mean, it's not like we're making out or *doing it* in public, but it might as well be like we are, with all of the sneers we've gotten in this town, all of the hate notes stuck to our lockers with gross chewed-up gum.

I want to move to Canada. I hear they're more tolerant of our kind there.

So we're walking arm in arm, *close*, and we're a couple of paces behind Greg Sherman, the most outspoken

Bible thumper at our school. He's striding ahead with his backpack slung over his shoulder (it has a WWJD patch ironed onto the front flap), and he's talking with Ed about Jesus or something, and then he's just suddenly...*not* there anymore. I mean, I wasn't looking at him—Celia and I were watching a really big heron or crane or something swooping way high up in the sky—but I know he *was* there, and the next think I know, there's just a pile of clothes on the sidewalk, no Greg in sight.

And, for that matter, no Ed, either. His jeans are crumpled on the cement where he stood, along with his socks, his boxer shorts, his shoes, his t-shirt boasting a "drummers do it in rhythm" phrase in neon yellow Comic Sans.

I only know this is the Rapture because my mom, back before she was Buddhist, before she was New Age, before she was Quaker, was a Born Again. Capital "B," capital "A." You know the type: if they could just *talk* to you about Jesus, if you'd just *listen* to what they had to say, you could be *saved* and spared from an eternity of torment. Et cetera, et cetera. She was only a Born Again for about a week; they were really hard on her about the pot habit. But she told me all about the Rapture, told me how, when it first starts to happen, the *true* Christians' clothing—their profane, earthly belongings—will be left behind, and the good, pious people who wore them will have disappeared, *zapped* right up to the safety of heaven, where they'll perch and stare down at the rest of us lowly worms while we while away the Tribulation.

Celia stares for a very long moment at the personless piles of clothes before she begins to scream.

I kind of just stare numbly. I mean, it's a fairy tale, right? Nothing in the Bible is *real*. They tell you that you can't wear polyester on Thursdays or some shit. Who could take that seriously? But here I am, we are, peering down at the vacated clothes of two I-guess-they-actually-

124

were-true Christians, and I have no clue what to do because the Rapture really…happened?

A black Prius rolls up and onto the sidewalk inches away from us, would have totally hit Celia if my neurons hadn't fired in that exact heartbeat, if I hadn't yanked her back. The car smashes into a telephone pole, and then the thing is sliding dangerously to the left, so I grab Celia's hand, and we run out of the way, out into the road, where another car is careening off the side because *there's no driver in it*, and I suppose there's a pile of clothes nestled on its driver's seat, and then the car runs into a tree and makes a metal-crunching sound that will probably haunt my nightmares for the rest of my life.

You know…if I have a rest of my life.

"What's happening, what's happening?" Celia asks, breath short, repeating the words over and over as if they're a mantra, as if the sound of them gives her comfort.

"It's okay, babe," I tell her, rubbing the small of her back, but my hand is shaking; we both know it's not okay. She just stares at me, beautiful blue eyes huge. "It's the Rapture," I hear myself saying, and then whisper, "fuck," whisper it again and again, because her eyes only get wider, and now she's crying, head in her hands.

"Oh, my god… Oh, my *god*. The Rapture?" She turns on me, face contorted with fear, with anger. "Kate, *seriously*?"

"I mean, what did you think it was?" I snap back. "Look at the clothes, Celia!" I crumple up and squat down and put my forehead on my knees, rocking back and forth. This can't be happening. This can't be happening…

I jump up when I hear the scrape of metal against tree again, and I reach for Celia's wrist. "No matter what's going on," I tell her quickly, "it's not safe out here. Let's go somewhere."

"Go where, Kate? It's two miles to my house,

three to yours…Where are we going to *go*?" she gasps, tears and mascara running down her face.

I take a deep breath and look around.

The gas station is deserted, a pile of stained uniform resting unhelpfully upon the countertop in the store—all that's left of Al, the attendant. I used to stop in here almost every day after school, buying stupid shit like Popsicles and candy bars and bubblegum. I creep down the aisles, Celia glued to my back, and we find another pile of clothes in the freezer section with a case of beer abandoned on the floor beside it, and I have this crazy moment where I hope for that thirsty bastard's sake that they serve his favorite brew in heaven. And then we're in the back room, and I'm locking the door behind us.

"Oh, my god, oh, my god," Celia wails, sinking into a chair. She shrugs out of her backpack—it thuds to the cement floor—and then her nails are raking through her dirty blonde hair, and she's crying, shoulders hunched up so high that they're level with her ears. I kneel down beside her, lean against the side of her chair, wrists on my knees.

I should say something. Do something. I don't know what to do.

"What…what happens after the Rapture?" asks Celia.

I take a deep breath, try to remember my mom's Born Again babblings. There was something about fire and brimstone, four horses, maybe a dragon, but I don't want to tell Celia any of that stuff, so all I say is "I don't know," but my voice rises up at the end, because I don't know if I don't know, and I don't know if I want to know…

"Oh, my god. What about Joey?" Celia asks then, gripping the arms of her chair. She unclips her cell phone from her hip and punches at it, then tosses it to the floor, cracking the case. "It's dead!" she wails. I pull out my own phone and pale; it's dead, too.

"Oh, my god, Kate, I have to go home. I have to see if Joey's okay."

"It's two miles to your house—"

"But he's my baby brother!" Her eyes are wild, like they get just before she takes a Geometry test, and I know I have to calm her down or she'll go into full-on panic mode.

"Listen, Celia, if Joey's not at your house—safe, indoors—then he's in heaven, where he's, I can only assume, pretty okay." I run my hands through my hair, and Celia stares at me for a solid minute before her face crumples. "Oh, babe, I'm sorry… But it's two miles, like you said, and I just think we should wait here for a little while longer—"

"What are we waiting for, Kate?" she sobs. "*We're* obviously not getting Raptured."

"Obviously," I murmur, rubbing at my eyes. I mean, we're dykes, right? Recently-Raptured-Greg had no qualms about telling me that I would never be *saved* unless I repented of the sin of homosexuality, that god would hang a big "no vacancy" sign on those pearly gates while Satan stirred up an awesomely hot pot of punishment— just for me. Greg always looked so smug when he delivered his stupid lunchroom sermons, even when I threw my ketchup-stained napkins at his face.

God, it makes me *ill* to think that self-styled junior evangelist could have ever been right about *anything*.

"All right, all right," I sigh, standing up and dusting off my jeans. "We'll go check on Joey. And your mom." *And my mom*, I think, but don't add. There's no way my mom was Raptured.

My mom's awesome—don't get me wrong. But she's not exactly the Rapturing *type*. She grows weed in the basement under one of those grow lights, and she believes in reincarnation and never, ever eats dairy products. She's nothing like Greg. But Al was nothing like Greg, either. I never even knew he was Christian, though I guess religion isn't the sort of thing you'd typically discuss with a kid trading a sweaty handful of quarters for a sugar high.

Outside, there are more crashed cars, but what's weird is that there are no *people*. None at all. There are smoking messes of scrap metal; there are sprinklers whirring in empty yards, and the traffic lights still flash from green to yellow to red, but there's nobody in sight. That's what freaks me out the most: the absence of moms yelling at their kids, of kids yelling at each other, of bicyclists and skateboarders and old people walking their dogs. It's just strange. Like, skin-crawly strange. There are always people chatting on the sidewalks, driving on the streets, commuters and freshly licensed kids paying no mind to the thirty mile-per-hour residential speed limit.

Arm in arm, hip to hip—there's no one to hurl slurs at us now—Celia and I skulk down the street. I steal glimpses through the house windows, hoping to spot someone inside. I do see that fluffy white dog at the corner, chained to a tree and snarly as usual, and his high-pitched barks give me a little bit of comfort, weirdly enough.

But he's the only living thing in sight.

"What if..." says Celia, after awhile, voice broken, shaking. "What if everyone's just...playing a prank on us?"

I blink a couple of times and shake my head. We pass by a truck mangled around a mailbox.

"I don't know! I don't know!" Celia yells then, shattering the silence and kicking a thick piece of broken windshield over the sidewalk with her sneaker. "But this can't possibly be real. Can it? I mean, seriously, *everyone* turned all harps and haloes, got Raptured straight up to heaven, except for *us*? What did we do wrong? What could we *possibly* have done that was so wrong?" She stops and turns toward me, lets her head fall down to rest against my shoulder.

I wrap my arms around her and take a deep breath. "It'll be okay, babe," I say, and I try to mean it this time. "We'll find some people. Don't worry. I'm sure they haven't *all* been Raptured." And of course I'm not sure of any such thing, but I still say it—to make her feel better. To make me feel better. But, really, who am I kidding? This is the end of the world.

"What if..." Celia's hyperventilating a little, clawing at my shirt. "What if we're the last people on earth?"

I hold her closer, hold my tongue, because I don't know anything. *I don't know.*

We separate—Celia's chin sags down to her chest—and we link arms again and walk a little farther in silence.

It's because we're walking in silence that we hear it: a sort of falling whine, like a bomb, like a whistle, a high-pitched howl. It makes me shiver, and right away I look up, we both look up, because you always look up at that kind of sound.

There's something bright and shining in the sky. It's light-colored, metallic maybe, and it's coming down, drawing closer to us. No. It's not drawing closer to us; it's going to miss us by a long shot, and I thought it was going to hit us because it's so huge. It looks small only from far away. It's then that I realize it's a plane, crashing.

The explosion, on impact, is deafening. I fall to the ground, smack my hands over my ears and squeeze my eyes shut, but the blasts seem to go on forever and ever, and we're both crouching, moaning, huddled together. The crash was far off, I think, but it sounds close, too close.

I look around, scanning for debris, and then I look up, and my heart stops.

More shapes hover in the sky. Hundreds of them, *thousands* of them. I tilt onto my side, leaning on my hands, gaping and squinting up, because they're not planes, not anything like planes, though for a long, terrifying moment, I think they might be planes. But then I reason with myself: how could they be planes? There could never be so many planes above us. I don't know if that many airplanes *exist* in the whole world. As the things draw closer, they become lighter and lighter in color, brighter, whiter, and then I can make out wing-like forms, and I wonder if maybe they are planes, after all, smaller planes, but no, they're not planes—*oh, my god*, they can't possibly be what I think they are…

"Angels?" whispers Celia, her voice hushed with awe as she stoops beside me. "Oh, my god, Kate. Are those angels? I think they're angels!"

I shake my head in disbelief, not to disagree, because I don't disagree, but… *Angels?* Seriously— *angels?*

As they loom downward, though, drawing closer in their freefall, I know. I stare at their gigantic wings, the fierce whiteness of the glowing light that surrounds them.

Yeah.

They're fucking angels.

Dread licks along my bones. I grab Celia's hand, and we run.

"Kate, what are you doing? They're *angels*!" she huffs behind me, but I shake my head, pant over my shoulder, "Celia, I'm pretty sure that some supremely bad shit is supposed to happen to the people who weren't Raptured. I'm not sticking around to find out what these angels have to say."

"But what if they're trying to Rapture *us*?" Celia asks, even though she's running faster now, no longer dragging her feet.

"I wouldn't count on it," I mutter, then duck as an angel swoops over us, alights upon the street and then zips up, hovering just above the ground. We don't stop running, though Celia's hyperventilating again; I squeeze her hand tighter. But I can't tear my eyes from it, the angel: it looks kind of a like an Oscar statue, no clothes, all smooth and golden, light and fire licking over its skin. I assume it's skin. And the wings burn, crackling. They don't flap so much as…blur.

Terror seizes me.

We angle into a random driveway, race toward the house. But I groan in frustration because the front door's locked, so we dash into the backyard, and I trip over a rainbow beach ball as we run past the in-ground pool, past the chaise lounge and the pair of dripping swim shorts, and then we're in the house, because—thank *god*, or whoever—the back door was open.

It takes a moment for my eyes to adjust to the dimness of indoors. I *was* just staring at a burning angel, after all. But then Celia is hissing at me from the living room, and I follow her in there, stare through the enormous picture window facing the road. The angel is floating across the lawn, right toward us. It moves faster than a blink, and I don't know what it's going to do, but it can't be nice, what it has planned, because it's blazing; fire undulates over its smooth body, hypnotizing me.

It's going to come through the glass, I know it. It *has* to see us standing here, frozen in place like rabbits, but it stops in front of the window and abruptly turns, blurring again, moving away from the house, from us.

That's when the screaming starts.

Celia and I look at each other, eyes wide, mouths open; my heart pounds so hard, I can feel it in my feet. Because it's a human scream, but I've never heard a scream like that… The worst scream I ever heard was in a haunted house in the fifth grade. My cousin Brad let loose this shrill, ear-shattering scream when a goblin-thing groped him in the dark, and he wet himself. This scream is worse than that: it's pitiful, hopeless, high and thin, and I think it belongs to a man. In silent agreement, Celia and I press our faces to the picture window, look out.

The angel's holding him up by one arm. The guy dangles about twenty feet above the pavement as the angel grasps his wrist with searing hands. He's kicking, the man, writhing in mid-air. He's middle aged, wearing a nice suit, and his screaming mouth is open too wide—it's grotesque—and another angel floats up beside him, cocking its bare golden head.

The angels don't seem to have real eyes, just twin burning holes, and they don't have real mouths, just firm, closed, unyielding lines, but as this second angel takes the man's other arm, an expression flits over its gleaming face, almost like…enjoyment. I swear its mouth curls up on one side.

The angels rip the man in half.

Oh, my god. They ripped him in *half.*

Blood splatters onto the pavement, and then the man's body, like meat, smacks the hard ground. The angels, still aloft, gaze down at the carnage, their fire eyes burning, and I'm not exactly sure what happens, but suddenly the man's body isn't there anymore. All that's left is his clothes.

I don't think he was Raptured.

Celia begins to cry very quietly, her hands over her mouth, muffling her sobs. I wrap an arm around her, drag her back from the window. My hand finds a doorknob behind me and turns. It's a closet, but it's pretty neat and clean for a closet—nothing like the closets at my house—so there's enough space for both of us to wedge ourselves inside. We press back and into it and close the door.

"Oh, my god, oh, my god, they killed him, oh, my

god," Celia says, her voice husky with tears. She's wrapped in my arms, shaking, and I'm shaking, too, and I can't seem to relax my eyes; they're still round as saucers. We just saw a man get torn in two—by *angels*—and everyone else is dead and gone.

Is this the Tribulation? Are angels supposed to come in the Tribulation? Oh, my god, what I'd give for a fucking Bible right now.

I hold Celia close, and she finally stops whispering to herself. I listen for outside noises, wondering if it's safe enough to venture out of the closet to try to find a Bible. Don't most houses have one? Even my own house has one, as a souvenir from Mom's adventures in religion.

"What are we going to do?" Celia asks, and she repeats it a few times for good measure. I stare at her, at her outline in the dark. She's asking me what we're supposed to do, but I don't know. I'm afraid of those angels. I don't *know* what to do, don't know how to deal with any of this, but Celia needs me, and I breathe out, try to breathe, kind of fail at breathing because my heart is hammering too fast, stealing my air away.

"Maybe we'll go check on Joey, yeah?" I whisper, and she's nodding against me, tears wet against my neck. "We'll…" I swallow, but my throat is too dry. "We'll go…outside, and we'll run—run really fast—and we'll make certain our families are fine, safe, and then…" I cough. "We'll figure the rest out later."

"I'm so afraid to go outside." Her voice is a whimper.

"We'll be careful," I say, and I sound a lot more confident than I feel.

But my hand's on the doorknob, and we tumble out of the closet, clinging to each other, and then we're creeping toward the picture window on our hands and knees.

I peek up over the edge the sill. Nothing. Nothing

shining, golden, burning. Just a couple of crashed cars and a sprinkler making its rounds.

"Let's go," I whisper, and Celia slides her hand into mine.

On our way toward the back door, I spy a set of keys hanging from a hook on the kitchen wall. There's a car parked in the driveway, and part of me wants to grab the keys and take the car, but the other part? Yeah, I know it's stupid, but what if this is some kind of mass hallucination? I'm desperate, clinging to anything right now, anything that feeds my teeny-tiny hope that *none of this is really happening.* And if I take that car, and if there are no consequences to taking that car, then this is all really real: the pious are gone, saved, and fire angels have come to kill the sinners.

I'm clinging to the last hope I have. And I'm going to keep clinging to it. Hey, maybe this is all just a bad dream.

"We're going to try to stay out of sight," I tell Celia when we step over the threshold and stand beneath the awning on the back porch. "We don't know how carefully they're looking for people, or if they're even looking for people..." I trail off, noting her vacant expression, the tears standing in her eyes. "Are you ready?"

Her chest rises and falls, and, lower lip trembling, she nods.

"Let's just go." I take her hand. It's slick with sweat, like mine, so I entwine my fingers with hers so she won't slip away. Without another thought, we're down the driveway, running along the sidewalk. So much for low visibility.

At least they make a sound, don't they? Or...wait. Was it the plane that made the sound? Everything is hazy in my head. My heart's pounding too fast, the blood rushing through my body. I'm not really a runner, and neither is Celia, but we're running fast, and my lungs are burning, and I just want to get home, get Celia home.

Nothing happens. I'm strung so tight, I feel like I'm going to snap, but absolutely, positively nothing happens as we sprint past blocks and blocks of the neighborhood. We even stop a few times, panting, sides heaving. And nothing continues to happen.

When we get to Celia's house, she moans—"No, no, no…"—crumpling on the front lawn, wheezing for breath and putting her head between her knees.

There's no car in the driveway. Her mom isn't home, and that means Joey isn't home, either. They could be anywhere. They could even be…

My eyes flick up toward the sky involuntarily. It's empty, save for some incongruous fluffy puffs of cloud.

"Kate, I just…" Eyes closed, Celia curls up on the grass, and her tears seep into the ground. "I just want to lay here. I can't—"

"No, babe, let's go inside. You can rest inside." I dare another glance at the sky before kneeling down to lift her to her feet. She wraps her arm around my shoulders, leans her weight into my side. Celia left her backpack at the gas station, along with her keys, so we head around to the rear of the house. Her mom never locks the back door.

It's surreal, stepping into the kitchen. The crock pot's on, and whatever's cooking smells delicious, but Celia yanks the plug out of the wall and presses her hand to the counter, staring at me, eyes wild, wide.

Everything's normal here. Nothing's out of place. Nothing's missing. There aren't any piles of clothes or smashed, smoldering cars, and there are no eight-foot-tall angels with burning, vibrating wings eager to tear us apart.

It's all been a dream, a nightmare. *Surely* it's just been a really fucking weird, horrible dream. But when we move through the house, take the stairs up to Celia's room and look through her yellow-curtained window, we see a blue pickup wrecked against the side of the neighbor's house.

It's real.

Together, we sit down on the edge of the bed, legs touching, and I think about all of the time we've spent in this room, remember when I came up here for the first time.

School's hell, but with our families, we've been really fucking lucky. Lucas Taylor, a kid in our grade, is gay, too, but his parents were so awful to him, he had to move into a youth shelter. My mom and Celia's mom have been totally supportive.

Celia's mom—Mrs. P, as she likes to be called—invited me over herself when Celia and I started dating, and when Celia took me upstairs to "show me her room," her mom got all super-excited, said she could hold dinner off. And I told her, "No, Mrs. P, it's not gonna be like that," but she giggled and said she remembered what being seventeen was like, which was a little weird—more than a little weird—but you'd just have to know Mrs. P.

So she waved us along, and I remember sitting side by side on Celia's bed; our legs were touching just as they are now. Celia took my hand and threaded my fingers through her own, and she leaned her head on my shoulder and sighed, and I remember thinking that the room smelled like peppermint toothpaste and lavender laundry detergent, because Celia had just brushed her teeth and changed her shirt (she was pretty nervous, having me over at her place). And I remember how she leaned over and kissed me. She was so shy; our lips barely grazed, but she tasted sweet, like a candy cane. I'll never forget the smile she gave me afterward. It was different from her school smile or her friends smile or her family smile. It was my smile.

Now she's pale and shuddering, teeth chattering despite the heat. I breathe out and grimly wonder: will

Celia ever smile again?

Her mom isn't here. Joey isn't here. I still have to find out if my mom's okay, but I suppose Celia should stay, in case her family...comes home? Is it possible that they could come home? And, anyway, she'll be safe in here. Indoors. I think. I don't know.

My pulse hammers in my temples, and my head aches. I'm so thirsty; my tongue is totally dry. I push some hair back from my face and stare at my hand for a second, stunned by how much it's shaking. I feel like Celia did out there on her front lawn. I want to lay down and never get up again.

I take a deep breath.

"I have to go check on my mom," I say—or croak, because my throat is so hoarse. I stand up. But Celia scrabbles at my hand, my arm, clings to me. "I think you should stay here, babe..." I begin, but she's shaking her head.

"No, no, I want to stay with you," she says, and I realize that there are no tears on her face, none poised to fall from her eyes. She stares up at me, looking so small, so vulnerable, so determined. "I've *got* to stay with you," she says, softer this time, and I feel my heart crumble into a thousand pieces and reassemble itself.

"All right," I tell her, breathing out. "We'll come back here, then. After."

Normally, the way to my house seems long after I drop Celia off on my walk home from school. But today it passes in a heartbeat. We're at Celia's house, and then we're in the driveway of mine, and there's no car in the driveway here, either, and when I unlock the front door and we step inside, there's a note on the counter from Mom, saying she had gone to the grocery store to pick up some things, and then she was going to stop at the bookstore on her way home, just to "browse." "Browse," of course, is code for "buy you some birthday gifts." My birthday is in a couple of days.

I crumple the note. I hold it in my hand, and I crush it between my fingers, feeling my own tears fall now, hot on my face. My mom isn't perfect, but I fucking love her, and she's not *here*, and I doubt she was Raptured, and I don't know what's happened to her... Have the angels gotten her? Such a tiny, tiny errand, and she might be dead now, and I don't know, I don't *know*, and it's mind numbing, this pain of not knowing.

I find a piece of paper and, with a shaking hand, write her a note: "Mom, I hope you're okay. I'm with Celia at her house. I'll come back to see if you're here tomorrow. Love, me."

It doesn't seem like enough, so I scrawl on the bottom, "I love you." I tape the paper to the counter, and then I'm taking Celia's hand, and we're leaving, shutting and locking the door behind us. I have to just believe my mom will come back safe and sound. I have to.

"Okay," I say, when we're standing on the porch. "Look...We've got to figure out what's going on. If this really is the Rapture, like we think it is, maybe we should go to...a church."

Celia gives me the same look I'm internally giving myself: *Seriously? Us, in a church?* But it's the only idea I have, and I guess she doesn't have any better ideas, because, finally, she sighs and nods.

"How about the one on the corner?" She jerks her chin toward it, and I breathe out.

"Yeah. Sure. It's as good as any."

My Social Studies teacher once said that people congregated in churches during the bombings of WWII. For some reason, I remember that, and it makes a weird kind of sense right now, in our current circumstances.

The church is only a hundred feet or so away, and as we get closer, we both freeze, because we hear voices. Normal voices. They're not screaming voices or frantic, terrified voices… We exchange a quick look.

"There are people in there," Celia whispers.

I nod my head, swallowing, afraid to hope. "Come on."

Hand in hand, we walk up the steps, edge inside, and stare into the sanctuary.

Oh, my god.

There are *people* in the church. Tons of people.

The place is *packed.*

I almost smile, I'm so relieved, but my mouth won't quite cooperate. Celia and I scoot into the back pew, and that's when the relief starts to wear off and I begin to feel kind of nervous and self-conscious, as I look around, take in the faces. I recognize some of these people, saw them protesting with giant poster board signs at the last Pride parade. Not that that is, you know, especially *relevant* in an end-of-the-world situation, but I think Celia remembers them, too, because she doesn't press her leg against mine.

There's a woman standing at the front of the church, wearing a white pastor-type robe. She's holding her hands out toward the congregation, and I suddenly realize that everyone's gone quiet, and all of their heads are bowed, and *I'm* not going to bow my head, but that's when it hits me. I don't know why I didn't make the connection before. If all of these people are Christians, why weren't they Raptured?

"We have come to the end times!" the lady at the front erupts, and everyone startles and shifts, including us. "Our friends and families have been taken to heaven, as the good Lord promised us in the Bible, and now we, the left behind, wait! Have you seen the angels?" She points high above her head. "They are here to bless us, to carry us with them to heaven!"

Some of the people start fidgeting in their seats. One woman raises her hand, but the pastor lady ignores her.

"The angels are tearing apart the wicked!" she announces, raising her voice. "They will not do so to us, the good people, the good Christians, the Lord's children!"

More hands shoot up in the air, too many for her to overlook now, so she sighs and shakes her head but waves her arm at a man near the front. He stands, hat gripped in his hands.

"Reverend Thomas, it's not that I don't believe you," he says quietly. I have to strain to hear him. "But the...the angels..." He chokes on the last word. "They tore my *wife* apart. Right in front of me." He holds up his shaking hands, and I'm sure I'm going to be sick, because they're covered in dried blood. "She was a good Christian, Reverend, and I don't think—"

"If she was a good Christian, then she is now in heaven," insists the reverend, pronouncing the words slowly, as if she's speaking to a small, stupid child. "So you need no longer worry about her. You need to worry about your *own* repentance, and what the Lord is going to do to you if you *don't* repent! We need to be repenting, people, here and now, and we need to do it with all of our hearts, and then we're going to go outside—all of us, go right out that door." She stabs her finger toward the back of the church. "And we're going to *ask* the angels of the Lord to come down and, in his infinite mercy, take us up to heaven!"

"How do you know that's going to work?" someone shouts.

"But what if we get killed?"

"But what if—"

"*Do you have no faith?*" the reverend bellows. "Have faith, and all will be well, and you will be granted your eternal reward. Let us pray."

Celia catches my eye; she looks stunned as she shakes her head back and forth. I mouth, "I know," and shake my head, too. We're not going to go outside and ask those bloodthirsty angels to come down and get us. But everyone else is silently praying, and then they're standing, shifting from foot to foot as Reverend Thomas strides down the center aisle and walks right through the double doors.

"Come and be taken up by the Lord!" she shouts, raising her arms over her head. The sleeves of her white robe hang low; they look like wings, and I shiver at the sight. She's outside, but we can still see her, standing there at the top of the steps. A few of the people follow her, anxiously standing beside her, kind of flinching up at the sky, but everybody else stays inside, turning to face the doorway, looking terrified.

"Oh, ye of little faith!" The reverend aims hooked fingers toward those of us staring out at her. And then she directs her face to the heavens, and this look of pure joy washes over it. "They're coming!" she calls out in a singsong voice. My heart beats double time as I watch the reverend and the people standing beside her reach toward the sky with their arms outstretched, like little kids begging to be picked up.

An angel swoops down beside Reverend Thomas. It doesn't stand upon the ground but floats a few feet above it, and it leans toward her, and she shrinks back a little, but she's still smiling when it holds out its arms, all motherly. She moves into its embrace, and then the angel is lifting, lifting, lifting her up.

I watch as every one of the people standing outside is lifted up by his or her own personal angel, and the reverend, floating several feet above the ground now, calls out to us, saintly smile on her face: "They have come to carry me to the kingdom of heaven! Hurry, believers! Come out, and you will be saved!"

A few men and women in the sanctuary take halting steps toward the doorway, wary. The angels hover just outside, holding their people carefully, tenderly. Celia turns to me with a questioning expression: *What's going on?*

But we jolt and lean against each other when the screaming starts.

I don't want to look, but I can't stop myself. The angel holding the reverend is...squeezing her in an embrace that's far too tight, and the reverend lets out a hiss, like that terrible sound an inflated balloon makes when you pinch its mouth but still let a little air escape.

I can hear her ribs cracking.

And then all of the angels are squeezing, and all of their passengers are wailing, and then there's blood, and the people in the church are screaming, stampeding, and I have one very clear thought in this horrific moment, and I know, without doubt, that it's true.

This isn't the Rapture.

It's something else entirely.

The golden things kind of look like angels, yeah, but are they, really? Or are they just monsters?

I sling my arm around Celia's waist and hug her close, ducked behind one of the pillars holding up the church. We're standing on the pew, safe from the people pushing and trampling each other to get away from the open doors, from the carnage happening outside. Someone shuts the doors then, but that scarcely muffles the awful sounds of people breaking and dying in midair.

There's a long moment—or maybe a short moment; I can't tell anymore—in which everyone seems to still, listening, breath held, waiting.

Then the sounds stop. There's silence outside. And I'm not sure if that's a good thing, if I should feel relieved or terrified.

The sanctuary is hushed. Will the angels come in after us now? Could simple closed doors deter them? They aren't even locked. I scramble down off the pew, realizing it at the same moment as someone else does, because we both stumble to the doors, me and this middle-aged guy in a backwards baseball cap, and we slide the bolts in place with a too-loud snap.

More quiet, more waiting. A woman near the pulpit is trying very hard to stifle her sobs but is quickly shushed by the people standing beside her.

It's painful, this waiting. All of the windows are stained glass; I can't see anything outside. Who thought that was such a great idea, windows that you can't see through? Suddenly I'm angry at the window-makers, at the architects of this church, because I need someone to be angry at, and they're probably all long dead, and they *never* could have planned for this, but I'm still mad—illogically mad—that they didn't take rampaging angels into account.

I'm standing with Celia, and we keep waiting, because waiting is better than being torn apart or squeezed to death by winged monsters. I keep rubbing Celia's back; it seems to soothe her. She's leaning against me, and she's still shaking, but she's breathing easier and doesn't look quite so pale.

Finally, startlingly, an older woman with dark hair shot through with grey stands up and jerks her thumb toward the doors. "I have to get out, have to see if my husband's all right," she says, voice raw. "I have to go, whether they're…whether they're out there or not." So brave, I think, and the guy who locked the doors with me moves toward them again, and I do, too, and together we unbolt the locks, and—because you have to, because how could you not?—we both peer out.

There's blood on the pavement, but there are no bodies, no body parts. Just clothes, and the reverend's robe. No angels in sight.

Murmuring builds in the church as the dark-haired woman, without hesitation, squeezes past us. We bolt the doors again.

The man in the baseball cap turns to me, his expression somber. "They can't be angels. No angel of god would *do* something like that." His eyes are intense, and he holds my gaze, as if he's trying to convince me, waiting for me to agree. "I don't think god has anything to do with this."

"Yeah. Neither do I," I mutter, taking a deep breath.

But if this isn't the Rapture, what is it? Where did those things come from, and why are they doing this?

People are whispering now, talking amongst themselves, and I don't think anyone knows what's really happening, and, anyway—does it matter? All of those people are dead and gone because they believed they were going to heaven. I hope to hell they got there, one way or another.

"What should we do?" Celia asks me then, meeting me in front of the doors. I push my hands through my hair, bunching it into a bun at the nape of my neck, and breathe out. I had hoped we would find help here. But I was wrong.

We haven't heard any screaming, any tearing or wailing from outside, so that woman must be all right.

"Let's go back to your house," I say, and Celia nods, and then we're opening up the doors and moving through them before we can change our minds. The doors shut fast behind us, and the murmuring voices are muffled, lost, like a dream.

We hold hands and stick to the overhang of the church for a long moment, scanning the sky. That's where they come from, and it seems so random, how they come, what they come for, so it's not like we could predict their next…attack.

I squeeze Celia's hand, and we trip down the steps and run along the sidewalk, moving as quickly as we can.

It's amazing how much faster you can run when you're terrified.

Just a hundred feet to my house, and there's no car in the driveway, but I want to check, just in case Mom came home on foot. She could have. I wouldn't drive a car with those crazy, fiery things falling out of the sky. But when the door is unlocked, when the house feels just as empty as before, when no one answers my shouts, a dragging heaviness weights down my chest, and the fear becomes real in my heart: I don't know if I'm ever going to see my mother again.

Celia hugs me gently from behind.

We keep running, covering the miles to Celia's house in less time than I would have ever believed possible, and then we're inside, and we lock the back door, push the kitchen table under the knob for good measure.

It feels as empty here as my house did, but Celia calls out for her mom, for Joey, and her voice kind of echoes, but no one calls back. Her face falls, but she shakes her head and takes a deep breath.

Together we move into the living room, just stand there and stare at one another for a really long time. Neither of us has any clue as to what's going on, but we're in the house now, and we're safe. Maybe we're safe.

"The television," Celia whispers, and I widen my eyes at her, mouth hanging open. It's so obvious—maybe it was *too* obvious, too normal to occur to us before—but surely someone's covering this on the news. Maybe they know what's going on.

"Yes! Where's the remote?" I say, a little too loudly, but Celia already has it in her hand, and the big flat screen over the mantel sizzles to life.

But there's no picture, just snow. Celia flips through the channels, through every single channel, hand shaking, but they're all the same.

We gaze at each other forlornly. No phones, no

television. And Celia doesn't have the Internet at her house.

"I'm hungry," she says then, in a soft, strange voice, and she turns around, walks into the kitchen, opens the fridge. I follow behind. I'm surprised that the light in the refrigerator comes on, that it's still making that soft *whirring* sound. I guess I figured that if the phones and TVs were switched off, dead, the refrigerator would be dead, too. It seems weird that it isn't.

And then I laugh—not a real laugh, not a good kind of laugh—because the fridge being on seems *weird* to me now? Oh, my god. I sit down at the stool by the counter, and I put my head in my hands, and I can't help it; I'm crying.

We're fucked.

No. I don't know if that's true. Not really. But it seems like we are. It really, really seems like we are. So, there's food in the fridge, and I hope that the tap is working, but how long will these things hold out? How much food does Celia's mother keep in the cupboards? Where are our parents? Where's Joey? What's happening? Does god have anything to do with this? I don't think he has anything to do with this. It all seems so random and so dark and really, infinitely terrifying, like we're on some haunted carnival ride that will never, ever stop.

Please make it stop.

Celia doesn't know I'm crying. She's making us sandwiches. I wipe my face and gaze at her, bleary-eyed, as she spreads the mustard perfectly thin and neat with a butter knife. She tears off chunks of iceberg lettuce, layers that on, and then she adds a few slices of bologna, starts to add some more but then seems to think better of it, slides them back into the package. I watch her do this, watch her mouth, the way it's turned into a deep, deep frown.

She sets my plate in front of me, and it makes a

hard click against the countertop, and we both jump, then kind of grin apologetically at one another. Celia sits on the stool beside me, and we begin to eat, but we take small bites, and half of my sandwich remains on the plate, and I'm staring out the window at the lowering sun, its red light reflecting off of the leaves of the big tree in Celia's backyard, and I'm wondering again if any of this is real, if it's happening, if it's a dream. But I know better now than to go look for the crumpled cars out on the street.

Evening comes, trailing shadows long and languorous in its wake. We're sitting together on the couch, silent, and we've seen no one—no people, no cars, no angels. Or, no, not angels. Monsters. I have to stop thinking of them as angels.

But as the sun sets, as the little fireflies start to appear, tiny flashing lights that startle me every time I see them (I keep mistaking them for people, or flashlights, or I don't know what), I think about how the school year is almost over. *Was* almost over. The end of the world is as good a reason as any to cancel classes. And I'm thinking about how my mom told me the fireflies are early this year because of global warming. And how I always equated global warming with the end of the world.

I never imagined the end of the world would be like this.

Clarice is the bag lady from up the street. She's not really a bag lady; she's actually kind of rich, but she's older, and I guess her mind is drifting, because she shuffles around the neighborhood, pushing her little wheely cart ahead of her, picking up random stuff—fast food bags, discarded sneakers, road kill—that she then stacks in neat, categorized piles on her front lawn. Celia once suggested that maybe Clarice is just environmentally conscious, just cleaning up the trash.

I have my doubts.

As we stare, glassy-eyed, out of the front window

now, Clarice comes wheeling her cart along the sidewalk, her face calm and relaxed, as if it's the most natural thing in the world to scavenge around the wreckage of a car in a neighbor's flowerbed.

For some reason, I'm not surprised to see her, don't even react, even though we haven't seen any other people since we left the church.

It's so hot and stuffy in the house. I'm restless. I stand up and edge toward the door.

"Why don't we go outside?" I ask Celia, whose eyes get all big and round. She begins to shake her head. "Just for a little while," I say, gazing at Clarice, at the empty sky above her. "Just to—I don't know—get some fresh air."

Celia's reluctant at first, but maybe she's feeling as cooped up, trapped, as restless and reckless as me, because finally she gets up from the couch, takes my hand, and outside we go. It's comforting to be near somebody we sort of know, a familiar face, so we walk right up to Clarice and pause beside her. She trying to tug a plastic bag out of a little tree's branches. It's hopelessly tangled, so I rip it down and hold it out to her.

"Thank you, young lady," she tells me, with hardly a glance.

"Clarice," begins Celia, uncertainly. "Are you...okay?"

The old lady cocks her head to the side, eyes squinting in Celia's direction. "Are you trying to sell me something? Why wouldn't I be okay?"

Celia and I exchange a worried look. "Have you noticed..." she tries again, spreading her hands, indicating the mangled cars polka-dotting the street and the lawns.

But Clarice shakes her head. "I keep to myself and keep my own business to myself," she states proudly, as if everyone in the world might be wise to do the same.

"But it's... Clarice, it's the end of the world."

Celia's voice is shaking; she bites her lip.

Clarice stares down at the plastic bag in her hands, and then she looks up, looks right at the both of us.

"I don't believe in the end of the world," she says very clearly, lucidly. "I don't believe in god, and I don't believe in the devil, so if you're trying to convert me, young lady, you'll have to do a much better job than that." She jams the plastic bag into her cart, and it promptly blows out, caught up in a little gust of wind, and skids across a lawn. "If *you* think it's the end of the world," she tells us then, "it is. But I'm not gonna believe any such thing." She begins to wheel her cart away, and then glances back at us over her shoulder. "The stars—*that's* what *I* believe in. The stars will keep me safe," she mutters, and with that, she and her cart squeak off in the dusk.

"I told you she was senile," I mutter, but Celia has stepped away from me, and her arms are wrapped around her middle, and she's staring at the back of the old woman as she shuffles around the bend in the road.

"What do you think she meant—that if *we* think it's the end of the world, it is?" Celia asks me quietly.

I roll my eyes, snake my arm around her waist, drawing her closer as I look up at the sky, flinching a little at sight of the first star just now beginning to peek out of the purple veil.

"It's not like she's some oracle," I say, sighing. "She's just a sad old woman. I don't think it meant anything."

"It meant something to me," Celia says.

"Okay. But listen." I press my lips against her hair, dropping my voice to a whisper. "That thing she said about the stars… It gave me an idea. What if the angels don't come out at night? I mean, I don't know that for fact," I tell her quickly, "and I'm not going to take old Clarice's word for it, but we've been standing out here for, like, twenty minutes now and…" I wave my hands at the sky. "No angels."

"I don't think they're angels," Celia says, shivering, pressing closer to me.

"Even if they do come out at night, they'll be easier to spot in the dark." I shrug my shoulders. "Like the fireflies."

Celia nods her head slightly.

We stare up at the dimming sky in silence. There are a handful of stars twinkling now.

"I'm afraid, Kate," Celia says after a long moment. I sigh, my gaze sinking back down to earth. There are so many fireflies out now; the bushes look like they're full of constellations.

"I'm scared, too." I squeeze her tightly, the truth between us unfolding soft and dark.

"I want us to stay together," she whispers. It sounds like a question; her words curve upward at the end.

I gaze down at her, almost smile. "Of course we're going to stay together," I promise, feeling a wave of incongruous hope as I kiss her lightly on her cheek. Like a moth to light, she turns her face toward me, and then she's kissing me, locking her arms around my neck as if she'll never let go.

Indifferent and beautiful, the fireflies burn around us, brighter than a whole sky full of stars.

THE FOREVER STAR

She was responsible for the stars.

She rolled them in her hands, sparking, white-hot, and held them up to her scrutiny as they pulsed. They shone in her palm when they were new, when they were just made. She formed the stars, and she held them over her heart, and she placed them just so in the shade of their own gravity.

Her sisters built the galaxies and the planets and all manner of moons and satellites, shaping them around each star like a perfect construct.

In the beginning, the stars were always perfect.

She did not know how she had come to this place, what she and her sisters called the Garden. Sometimes they would swim out into the velvet black of the sky and *look back at their little home, a planet no bigger than the sprawling confines of the temple that rested upon it. They watched the rising and falling civilizations with great interest, and they could make and remake their temple as often as they liked in the style of the worlds they favored. They had developed a fondness for the architecture of the early Greeks on Earth, so their temple was now a heavy, impressive thing, white and many-columned.*

She was called Elaine, though she had not always been called Elaine, or anything at all. She had begged her sisters for a name. They had all begged each other, had all desired names in the style of the people they watched on faraway worlds. And so they had given themselves names in a solemn ceremony, making wreaths of stars to crown their heads, braiding planets and tailing comets into their manes. They had given her the name Elaine because it meant "light" in some Earth languages, and it seemed appropriate, to name the star-creator a luminous word.

But despite the brightness in her existence, and despite her sisters, Elaine was very lonely.

She watched different civilizations in different galaxies, watched as they formed and unformed, as stars were born and as stars died. She and her sisters kept making their stars and moons and galaxies and planets, but it seemed as if, just as quickly, entropy took hold of their perfection and ate it away, like rust to metal. Elaine watched her once-perfect stars wink out and implode, and she wondered: is this all there is?

She could not remember a time before she made the stars. She had simply appeared in the Garden with her sisters, and she knew that they were her sisters, just as naturally, as innately as she knew how to make stars.

But what did it all mean? *What did it mean, to watch the orbits of the planets and moons and then watch as, across the span of mortal time, it all disintegrated, lost* to the death of the star? Everything ended with the death of the star; that wounded Elaine the most. She despised watching something she'd loved so much, something she'd birthed in her own hands...perish.

One day or night or morning—one could never tell which, but Elaine liked to think in mortal terms—Elaine rose from her stardust-covered chair. Her sisters watched her wordlessly, pausing in their design of celestial bodies. Luna gazed at Elaine with her silver head tilted, holding in her hands an unfinished moon.

Elaine glanced from one to the other, stared at the star stuff in their palms, at the glitter of minerals beneath their feet. And she breathed out and said, "I am leaving."

The sisters blinked their shining eyes and stood, and Luna moved to Elaine, leaving her moon to roll upon the star-slick table. "You can't," she whispered. "If you go, everything will...stop."

"How do we know that it shouldn't stop?" argued Elaine. She had thought things over very carefully. For millennia, she had thought. All of the lost civilizations, all of the worlds that had been born only to wink out into darkness, forgotten... Did it matter? Did any of it matter? Who would notice if the cycle came to an end?

"This is what we are meant to do," said Terra, the planet builder. She crossed her arms solidly, shaking her head at her sister. "Elaine, you mustn't."

Elaine embraced each of her sisters in turn. "I am empty," she told them. "I do not know why I was created. I make stars, and they burn out and die. I am empty because my purpose is to make something that cannot endure, that will, inevitably, fail. I can no longer bear it. I must go. I'm afraid," she said, in a small voice, "that there will be nothing beyond this place for me, that I will be unmade, like my stars. But if I do not go, if I do not try, my heart will be unmade of its own accord."

The sisters exchanged glances but nodded their heads in resignation: they knew that Elaine's mind could not be persuaded.

"We will try to make the stars in your absence," said Luna. And then, "We will miss you," she whispered, kissing Elaine on the cheek.

And Elaine went to the edge of the marble balcony, peered down into the swirling vortex of stars and moons and galaxies and planets, and she leapt.

"Fuck the reactor," I mutter, punching the console; it flashes blearily in the dark. "Oh, fuck it, fuck it," I moan, as the beeping grows louder.

"Maggie, what *the hell* are you doing? We need it shut down yesterday!" Sarge bellows from below deck. "If you don't get it stabilized, I will personally cut out your liver and eat it in front of you!"

"You'd be poisoned!" I spit out at him. My fingers race over the keyboards. The beeping slows, quiets, until the whine of the emergency siren is silenced altogether.

I slump against the console and breathe out, shaking.

I hear Sarge on the metal ladder before I see him: it groans beneath his weight. When he swings up and onto the narrow bridge, I get a look at his face, and I feel the blood drain from mine.

"What happened?" I whisper.

He takes off his hat, mopping at his bald head with a dirty bandana that he shoves it into his back pocket, sighing.

"Too long. Too late. A little girl was burned," he mutters, refusing to meet my horrified gaze.

I swallow. "How badly burned?"

"Dead."

I'm not ready to die.

I rock back and forth on the stained chair in the control room. Back and forth, back and forth, perched on the very edge, my arms wrapped around my legs.

I sent off another message to Copper City. I can't get into contact with Gold or Silver, haven't heard from them in weeks. I don't want to think that Gold and Silver are gone. Can't think that.

I wait by the control panel, waiting for it to flash with an incoming message alert, waiting for it to do anything other than *nothing,* glowing that maddening, static red. But no lights flash, nothing changes, and I'm exhausted, drained, slumping in my chair.

Another one died today. I can't blame myself, because I used to blame myself, and that was unbearable. Besides, if I give in to the throes of grief and put myself out of commission, *everyone* will die, and then what will happen? Will it all just…end? Just like that?

I wipe away my tears—furiously—and I rise.

"Alex," I tell the woman seated at the panel beside me, "you'll come get me if Copper responds?"

"Yeah," she says, and gives me a watery smile. "You got it powered back on real quick, Mags. Don't let it get to you, okay?"

Yeah. Sure. Just another girl dead. Won't let it get to me.

I grunt at her, hook my thumbs in my belt loops, and leave the room.

I used to be a regular mechanic. I could repair everything: just show me a gadget with cogs and wires, and I'd get it working again. But then the sun happened.

The scientists—or whoever studies that sort of

155

thing—had known the sun was dying for three hundred years, but it was a slow, long-suffering death. We had plenty of time to prepare, to build great machines based off of reactors that could shield us from the sun, from the savage UV rays, from the blasting and suffocating heat.

But not everyone had the means to erect the shields—only the major cities. Which was all right, in the beginning. Because the cities also had the machines to make the food. We all knew the rules: we stayed beneath the shields, and we survived just fine, content and contained.

The solar flares were persistent, though. They were small and manageable at first, but then they got deadly. Solar flares fuck with the mechanisms, push them off kilter. Occasionally, the shields would fail.

And people would die. Quickly. Sometimes instantly. Burned alive.

Like the little girl today.

I rub my hands over my face. I can't think about her. Can't think about any of them. Yesterday, two women were incinerated.

There are advisories everywhere: don't step out of your building without a sun suit. But people rebel, because they're a prison, those suits. It's a prison, this dome. People still hope—despite common sense, despite all of the data—that they can stand outside, feel the heat on their unsuited skin, for five minutes. Surely, for just five minutes, they'll be okay. And then the reactor fails, and for just five minutes, the shield drops.

No matter how many precautions we take, no matter how fast we move to get everything operational again, *someone* always dies. Or several someones.

There are rumors circulating about Silver, that their shields faded eternally a couple of weeks ago. That everyone in the whole city perished in a matter of hours, the wordless heat rolling in like a battalion from hell.

There are similar whispers about Gold.

And Copper? Communication seems to have ceased with them, too.

If it's true, if Gold and Silver have burned, if Copper's gone, then Bronze's shields will surely fail soon. *Our* city, *our* shields. We'll lose the fight. We'll all die.

I'm not ready for death.

I walk down the street, hands buried deep in my pockets. But I'm a hypocrite: I didn't put on my sun suit, was too lost in thought to strap it on before I stepped outside. I realize that fact when I'm more than halfway to my apartment. It would take longer to go back than to keep moving forward.

I run down the deserted street, heart pounding. The reactor might fail at any second, any heartbeat, and if it fails, I will die.

Alex is a skilled mechanic, but we both know she's not as good as me, not as fast at fixes, and it scares us, though we never talk about it. She's more apt to panic, slower at getting the system cooled down and back online. Her deliberations have cost several people their lives.

So I take small breaks, and I ration my sleep, but I can't keep going like this. I feel half alive, usually forget to eat, rarely speak with anyone about anything besides the sun, and the reactor. And, hell, the reactor is deteriorating.

I don't want to die. I want to live so badly it hurts.

I jog along, glancing side to side as I always do, looking for...I don't know what. Something. Something I can never find.

But now I glimpse a shadow in an alley, a slouched shadow. It looks like a person, and I turn on my heel, cursing myself for my stupid curiosity. But what if it *is* a person? What if they were out during the last shield fail? What if they're hurt? Or worse?

I step into the alley.

It is a person, and she *does* look like she's hurt. I squat down next to her and, hesitant, turn her over. She's curled on her side, protecting her middle, and she's wearing strange clothes, white clothes. No sun suit. I feel for her pulse; she's alive, and that means she needs to be helped, saved, taken indoors *now*. I swing her up and over my shoulder, hear her groan a little. She's still unconscious, but that's far better than dead. Grunting under her weight, I turn and start to half-run, half-slump toward my apartment.

The door of the brick building slides opens when it recognizes my fingerprint, and then we're through the entryway and down the hall and in my room, number six. I kick the door shut behind us. The grey walls are cracked and peeling, and there's no furniture besides a broken couch—sagging from my uneasy, stolen naps.

I ease the woman down to the cushions and then take a step back from her, panting, trembling with relief. We survived, made it inside without sun suits. We're safe. I rake a hand through my hair and blink down at the unmoving, white-clad form.

She's not from around here.

Yeah, that's an understatement. In a city of no strangers, she's a fucking *stranger*. How is that possible? I kneel down next to her, and I prod her shoulder a little. No response. Her hair curls over her shoulders, and she's wearing a golden crown of leaves.

She's pretty.

Really pretty.

I poke her in the shoulder again—and again, harder, when she stirs.

"Hey," I say.

She opens her eyes, wide and silvery blue.

"Where…where am I?" she whispers, though I don't see her lips move. I blink and shake my head, stare down at her, clear my throat.

"Hey, you're awake. Are you okay? Where are you from? This is Bronze City. Where...did you think you were?" I shove my hands in my pockets.

She blinks then, gazing hard at nothing, as if she's thinking hard, trying to figure something out. "Bronze City?" Her lips do move this time, and she sits up, puts her hand to her forehead. She closes and opens her large eyes, and then she stares at me. I rock backward on my feet, self-conscious, as her gaze sweeps from me to the floor, to the walls, to the creaky couch beneath her. I flush.

I mean, it's not one of the *nicest* rooms in Bronze, but have I ever cared before? No. Shit, Maggie, why would you *care* now?

I clear my throat again.

If only she wasn't so damn pretty.

"What galaxy am I in?" she asks then. I almost laugh, but her expression is too serious.

I sigh, lean back on my boots. Pretty...and crazy. I kneel down before her, meet her gaze at eye level. "Okay, lady, are you part of the ops that the city's sending out? Are you involved in some experiment? Who are you with?"

She shakes her head, doesn't understand. Then she sits up, leans forward, her shining head cocked, and raises her hand. I flinch a little, surprised, when she traces her finger down the line of my cheek, over my jaw. I open my mouth, but I'm stunned to silence, and I shiver.

"You're softer than I thought you would be," she says then, sitting back, folding her hands in her lap. "I couldn't tell how people would feel...not from so far away."

I remain frozen before her, speechless.

She shudders a little after a moment and stands, moving fluidly to the window, where she stares out at the dome and, through the dome, to the sun.

"You're not supposed to look at it," I tell her, finding my tongue and rising to cross over to her, touching her arm. Her skin is softer than mine. What did she mean by "people"? People from Bronze City? Is she an escapee, a survivor from Silver or Gold or Copper?

"I can look at it, the star," she tells me quietly, watching the burning orb without blinking.

Sometimes, when you look up at the sun, you can see the solar flares hanging in the sky before they hit, before they strike the dome. There's one hanging there now.

I clear my throat. "Excuse me, but... Who exactly are you, and where exactly did you come from?"

She turns to me, pierces me with her mirror-like eyes.

"My sisters called me Elaine. What's your name?"

"Maggie," I tell her. "Maggie Terrence." I take a deep breath. "Look, lady—Elaine. Where did you come from?"

She turns to the sun again, rubbing at her arms distractedly.

"Up there," she whispers.

"Right." I frown and chew at my bottom lip, working my jaw. Elaine looks back to me, notes my expression.

"I'm the star maker," she explains quietly. "I make the stars, and my sisters make the galaxies and the worlds and the moons. Or...I *did* make the stars. I left." She gazes down at her naked feet upon the filthy carpet. "I watched too many stars die. I couldn't—"

"Well, okay," I interject, holding out my hands to her. "That's great to know. So now I'm just going to take you to City Hall, and the folks there can help you get back to wherever it is that—"

"No. There's no going back," she whispers, and

her eyes flash with an inner light. "Your star is dying, Maggie," she says, looking up toward the sky again. "It's old, and its cycle is ending."

"And you know this because…you made the star?" I ask, sighing. "Look—"

"There will be a terrible solar flare in a moment." She's watching me closely, eyes heavy lidded. "It will blow out that hard dome that you built over your city. It will blow out the windows if you don't shield them right now."

"Shield the windows?" I narrow my brows and rub at my eyes. "There are building shields, but they're not activated. They drain the power grid, and we need all the power we can get to enable the dome."

"You should activate them." Her voice is small but certain. And then, what gets me, what really gets me—she looks deeply into my eyes, her own wide and teary, and she speaks a single word: "Please."

I step out into the hallway and hotwire the breaker.

And the building's shields power up. Just as the dome collapses.

The sirens are deafening, but I still hear the children screaming upstairs. Hell, I can hear their mother screaming, men screaming. I can hear a thin yowling outside, and then a tragic nothingness.

I crouch down on the ground, covering my eyes against the brightness that the building's simple shields can't shade.

I count slowly, evenly, as my breath becomes ragged, as my heart stumbles in my chest, because the sirens are still wailing; the dome is still down.

Come on, Alex. Hurry…

When my count reaches 106, the sirens stop, though my ears still ring. I open my eyes.

Elaine stands at the window, her arms folded

around herself as she stares out.

"It's worse than I could have imagined," she whispers. "This suffering."

I flop down on the ground, willing myself not to weep. And I don't, but my sides heave for a long moment as I become aware of the solidity of the floor beneath me. My eyes are tightly closed. Then I get up, dust off my bottom and, because there's absolutely, positively nothing I could have done or could do to save anyone who fell victim to the flare, I cross over to the couch, and I sit down, resting my hands on my knees.

I keep my mind carefully blank.

Elaine comes near. She takes precise, gliding steps, like a dancer. I've never seen anyone move like her. And when she crouches in her white dress before me, gazes up at me, my feeble brain can't help but think, *Wow, she's pretty.* Those brilliant eyes... I'm doing my best not to stare at her décolletage, but the neckline of her gown swoops low. I rub at my face and look up at the cciling, crashing back to reality.

"How did you know?" I ask her then, eyes glued to my hands in my lap. "How did you know that flare was coming? Was there a sign? Did you see something in the sky that—"

"I told you," she said quietly. "I made that star. I know everything about it. I...feel it." She rests a hand against her chest. "Here."

I inhale deeply and swallow the lump in my throat. It's impossible, but I almost believe her for a second—she's so earnest, so steadfast—before I remember *facts* and *science*, and I get up and cross to the communicator patch on the wall. It rarely works after a flare, but I try it, anyway, pressing the button for the reactor control room. No static. Nothing.

"Why don't you believe me?" she asks then, standing, her hands folded in front of her. "Where do *you* think the star came from?"

I bluster for a moment, blinking. "Where do I— What—Is that even a question? The Chaos Explosion! Every school kid learns that." I run my hands through my hair, frustrated.

Elaine cocks her head. "The Chaos Explosion," she murmurs. "That is your creation story here?"

I just stare at her.

"I have gathered many different stories from many different planets and civilizations." Her expression is thoughtful. "But I like this one. It's a beautiful image, to envision an *explosion* of newborn stars." A shadow falls over her face, darkening her shining eyes. "But I did make the sun, and I know that it is dying. You have little time before a fatal solar flare will burn this sector of the planet." She looks up at me. "The dome will not be able to withstand it. It will be destroyed."

And we'll all die, I add silently.

I feel like a husk, like a machine that's powered down forever. I don't know if I should believe her; it's probably crazy to even consider believing her. But didn't she just predict that flare? And didn't I already know all of this, that it was only a matter of time before Bronze City met its ultimate fiery doom? Of course I knew this. But it's too soon. It will always be too soon. There's so much left undone. There's so much... There's just *so much*. I stare off into space, feel my heart, my dreams, my life falling away from me. Stolen by the star Elaine claims to have made.

She kneels down at my feet, her hands on my knees, her eyes wide and beseeching. "Maggie..." she begins, and then she changes her mind, bites back the words on the tip of her tongue, takes back her hands. I miss them. I liked the comfort of them, their weight.

"It doesn't matter who you really are, or who you think you are." I sigh and put my head in my hands. "I just didn't believe it would ever happen, not really. The end. I thought... I thought we'd have more time, that there'd always be more time."

Gold and Silver are gone. Obliterated. I know they are. It's stupid to deny it any longer. Copper is probably gone. And we're next. We're the last. But does being last matter when there's nothing left?

"Maggie." Her lips remake my name into something strange and shining. She reaches out and touches my knee with two long fingers, and I feel the heat within them. The heat of a sun, a star. "Maggie, I might be able to help you."

"Help me," I echo, and I don't know if it's a question or a plea. I sigh. She's beautiful, and she's very sincere, but we'll all be dead soon, according to her. There's no help for that, no way out.

But she's nodding her head. "I will help you," she insists. "I will help you because you were kind to me. You carried me. Brought me here."

I spread my hands, and that simple gesture exhausts me. "Well, you're welcome? I guess." I curl up on my side. "I just need to sleep, okay? You can sleep, too, if you'd like. Do whatever you'd like." And then I no longer care about anything—not about beautiful, star-making strangers or imminent death by fire—because I've sunk into the couch, my face pressed into the cushions, and all the terrors of the day congeal into one cold lump of darkness that smothers my consciousness.

I wake to the sound of crinkling.

I sit up fast, bolt upright, because there's never the sound of anything in my room unless the sirens are about to go off, unless the kids upstairs are crying, but then I remember what happened, remember Elaine, and I feel…strange.

I feel even stranger when I find Elaine sitting at my table, containers of food scattered around her, a spoon in one hand and a gallon of iced sugar in the other.

An empty gallon of iced sugar.

"Food is *remarkable*," she mumbles around a mouthful of something. She gets up and comes to me, holding out the spoon laden with curling pink. "You have to try this!" Her smile is so disarming, I actually take the spoon from her.

"What, did you eat everything in the cupboards?" I hobble over to the open cupboard doors and find them devoid of food canisters. "You ate everything in the cupboards!"

Elaine grins at me excitedly, nodding. "It was all—what is your word for it?" She closes her eyes for a long moment and then opens them wide. "Delicious. It was *delicious*. I have seen the lengths that civilizations have gone to to acquire food, and I thought it must be wonderful, and it truly is!"

I stare at her for a long moment before, silently, placing the spoon in the sink and rubbing the remnants of dreams from my eyes.

It's been a weird day.

I press the button for the reactor control room on the communicator patch and, with a sigh of relief, hear Alex's voice, crackling: "Maggie? Are you coming in?" She sounds wired tight. I lean against the wall and massage my shoulders, watching Elaine open a tube of cheese alternative.

"Yeah," I tell Alex quietly, "I'm coming. But I'm bringing in a…friend, too."

"Just get here," she stutters, breaking the connection.

I move to the closet and dig my hand around inside until my fingers close around a pair of old work overalls. I tug it out, look it over. There are holes at the knees, but it's serviceable enough. Paired with a faded blue shirt, it's sort of an outfit.

"You can't walk around like that, in that dress," I tell Elaine, who turns to me, wide-eyed, with fake cheese smeared on her cheek. "We don't wear stuff like that here. People will think… Well, they won't know what to think. Best not to draw attention."

"Right," she says, and begins to take off her dress.

"Uh," I say, looking away, holding the overalls and shirt out at arm's length, in her general direction. I'm blushing again, and, *really*, *Maggie, blushing?* I wouldn't be blushing so damn much if I didn't think she was so damn pretty, but there you go; it's out in the open: I'm attracted to her.

But I don't think she thinks like that. She's pulling on the overalls, and I'm still not looking at her, but then she walks over to me, holding out the clips. "Maggie, how do you…?" She stares down the bits of metal, perplexed.

And she didn't put the shirt on first.

"You just, you know, clip them together," I say, hands in my pockets, staring down at the ground.

"Oh. Is there anything wrong?" She leans down to catch my eye.

"No. Nothing's wrong." Well, besides that we're-all-going-to-die thing.

"Your face is very red."

I squeeze my eyes shut. I didn't get enough sleep for this.

"I think you're pretty," I admit, shrugging, the exact opposite of suave and seductive. "I don't often notice pretty things," I grumble, scratching the back of my neck. "I work hard, and I don't have time for…" I sigh. "But I guess I wanted you to know that I think you're pretty."

She's stopped what she's doing, and she looks down at herself for a moment, then lifts her gaze back up at me. "What does it mean," she asks then, "that you think I'm pretty?"

I cringe and lick my lips. "I don't know what—"

"Do you want to kiss me?" she persists, sounding excited. "Because, like food, I have seen civilizations do much to attain kissing. And...other things. I always liked the look of kissing, and I would like to try it."

I stare at her.

"Do you want to kiss me?" she asks again, softening her voice. Her eyes are so wide, so blue.

"I mean, yes, of course I do," I say all in a rush, because I *do*, and for whatever reason, it's easy to confess this truth to her. "But...kissing *means* something."

She stands before me half-dressed, tilting her head. "Love," she whispers. "That's what it means, doesn't it? That's the intangible thing that so many people pursue. Well..." She examines the clips again and tries to press them together. "Love and power and currency. But love is *one* of the most important things, I've noticed, as I watched the civilizations rise and watched them fall."

I shake my head at her. Guess she's still sticking to that star creator claim. "Anyway, Elaine, we just met. So we don't love each other."

At this, her expression turns pensive, and her hands still, the clips forgotten. "But can't it grow?" she asks me, eyes wide as moons. "Isn't that how it works, love? It grows. Over time."

"Well, yes, of course it grows—"

"So can't it grow between us?"

I open my mouth, but no words come out. This is absurd. I mean, yes, of course it *could* grow, over time, but we have no time. I soften as I stare at her, into her round eyes, her all-knowing eyes that somehow, at once, look so naïve.

"Things grow from seeds," she says calmly, reasonably. "So please kiss me, and we'll have planted the seed."

I shrug, and I decide not to over think it. I just step forward, and I put my arms about her waist. She's warm and soft, and as my fingers slide over her skin, a shiver spikes through me, top to toe. She loops her arms over my shoulders, twining her hands behind my neck, and she angles her mouth up to me, eyes half-closed.

We kiss.

She tastes sweet—well, she *did* just eat a tub of iced sugar—but it's more than that: warmth, that softness of mouth. There's a spark of heat, a great curling of color that spirals within me. When she leans back, smiling up at me, I'm surprised at how mischievous she looks, and how happy.

"That was better than I thought it would be, too," she tells me, touching my collar. "I am very glad I met you, Maggie Terrence."

I mumble something unintelligible, excuse myself to stumble into my room's wash pod. I stare at myself in the mirror and touch my mouth with one finger.

There's a glittering upon my lips. Like stardust.

I make her wear a suit. She doesn't want to, tells me that it's impossible for the star to burn her, since she created it, but I ask her to slip into it, anyway, *just in case*, and, eventually, she relents. Together, we walk down the streets, moving slowly in our bulky outfits, aimed toward the reactor.

There's no one else out, but through the building windows, I hear sobs. Wails.

I take a deep breath.

We march resolutely along until we finally reach

the main door of the reactor. I take off my gloves, swipe a fingertip over the reader, and then we're striding through dank, dark halls, where the whir of machinery is constant, like a background heartbeat. I hardly hear it anymore.

"Where have you been?" asks Alex, pounding down the hall toward us. There's sweat streaming down her forehead, beading on her neck, and she's got a welding helmet strapped on her head. "Oh, fuck, Maggie. It's bad."

"Bad," I repeat, instantly tense, on alert. "How bad? What happened?"

"Sarge…" she begins, and she's taking off the helmet, running her hand through her hair. She won't meet my eye.

"What about Sarge?" I whisper, and Alex drops the helmet, leaning over to clumsily pick it back up. She hasn't given Elaine a second glance.

"He was up on the roof when the flare hit, because he was repairing—"

"*Is he hurt?*" I hiss, hands balled into fists.

She's shaking. "He's at the burn hospital."

I turn, and I shed my suit, and then I'm out the door, running over the packed dirt toward the hospital. Elaine calls out behind me, and Alex is shouting something, but I don't hear them; I just keep running.

At the front door, a nurse with a clipboard meets me, shaking her head, lips pursed. "You can't go in. They're at max for visitors."

I run past her, and I'm through the double doors, and I slap my hand on the front desk.

"Sarge Terrence," I say to the seated nurse who looks up, startled, and drops her pen. "Where is he?"

"In the city unit," she tells me, and she's about to say something else, but I'm off, already down the hall, because of *course* he'd be in the city unit—what was I *thinking* even asking?—and my heart is pounding so hard,

I'm surprised it's not exploded out of my chest, and oh, fuck, oh, *fuck,* it can't be Sarge; he can't be hurt. It's *Sarge*. Sarge *doesn't get hurt.*

He's sprawled across the bed, feet dangling over the baseboard. His right arm and leg sport bright white casts, and his face is turned away from me, but his eye is open. I cross to the side of the bed. I'm going to sob, want to sob, but I can't, because he turns to me, mouth smiling like always…but this smile doesn't quite reach his eyes.

"What *the fuck* were you doing on the roof?" I ask him, and then I stop fighting it: I start crying.

"Shit, Mags, I didn't think you had tears in you," he tells me, and he sighs for a very long time.

I can't even look at him; every time I do, the pain is so intense that I forget to breathe. I can't imagine how badly he's hurting. I can't imagine how he's laying there in that bed without screaming in agony. But this is Sarge. He probably bullied the nurses into giving him more drugs. That'd be just like him.

"I'm gonna die," he tells me then. I ball my hands into fists, and I shake my head so hard and fast, I feel the world spinning.

"You can't, because we promised," I'm telling him, and I can hear someone enter the room, but I don't even look up, because nothing matters but right here and right now, and my stupid fucking father lying, dying on the bed.

"We promised we'd do what we could by the reactor," he rumbles, and I can hear how badly the burn got his lungs by the tremor behind those words. "It don't matter, anyway, Mags. The signal to Copper bounced back to us. They're all gone."

I sink down, squat on the ground, my head in my hands. I rock back on my heels, feel the solidity of the chipping, dirty floor beneath the soles of my boots. It's so strong, so stable, the floor, like it could never be moved, could never sink, fall, fail.

"Who's this pretty lady?" labors Sarge then, and I rise and gaze back at Elaine, who's standing in the doorway, hands clasped in front of her, looking from me to my father, and back to me again. "Come in, come in," he tells her, magnanimous as always, and she steps into the room, the door sliding shut behind her.

"Sarge, this is Elaine," I whisper, rubbing my knuckles over my eyes. I'm still crying, but quieter now, tears dripping down the side of my nose. Elaine comes over to my father, nods to him, and he looks up at her with this wide, wicked grin that does crease his eyes, just a little.

"Has my little girl found someone special?" he asks me, teasing, but I just sigh. I can't speak. Elaine, though, looks to me, turning her head, and she glances down at Sarge, at the casts and the wounds and the charred, bubbled skin, and she reaches out her hand and takes hold of his bare one.

Sarge jerks a little—the hand that's not in the cast is burned, too, but not as badly—and then he kind of deflates, sinks back down against the pillows, closing his eyes. He looks like he's drifting away, like he's *dying*, and I step forward, mouth open, heart a hammer, breaking my ribs, but then there's this flare of *light*, and I cover my eyes. There's a flare! We're going to die—

But in the next moment, I know: it's not a flare. It's not the sun.

It's *her.*

I stare at Elaine, squint at her, at her skin white and pulsing, white and hot, like the stars I see at night sometimes. She holds my father's hand, palm up, and in the center of his palm, beneath hers, there's a sphere of light that pulses, pulses…and disappears.

My father slumps back against the pillows again,

his body loose, limp.

His burns are gone.

His burns are gone.

Fuck. *Fuck.* I cross to him. I feel his pulse, and he's alive; he's okay. The casts just fall apart, fall off of him, and then there's his skin, just as it was a day ago, and *all of his burns are gone.* Healed.

Elaine has stopped pulsing, the light filtering through her gently, gradually, until she stands muted beside the bed, and she places my father's hand gently upon his stomach and steps back from his side. Her eyes are unfocused, distant, as if she's thinking about something very important. In the palm of her open hand floats a white, winking light that fades, too, until it's gone entirely.

Everything inside of me feels as if it's been broken and remade, shaped into something new and precious and *sharp.* I kneel down, my knees crunching sand and dirt against the floor of the tiles as I bow before Elaine. It's all I can think to do, and my tears nearly blind me, but I know she's looking at me, and I rub at my face and look at her: her irises glow.

"Thank you," I whisper. I don't know what else to say.

But for a short while more—minutes, an hour, a day? I'm afraid to ask, to know—I have my father. My gratitude is deeper than the sky.

Elaine puts her hand over her heart, shuddering, then gazes down at me and shakes her head. "Please don't," she breathes, and then she stumbles out of the room.

My father breathes evenly.

"Where is she?" I ask Alex, stepping into the

reactor's hall. She's trying to prop up my suit, and Elaine's, against the far wall.

"What?" she asks, shaking her head, and then I'm grabbing her shoulders, shaking her a little. I can't blame Alex for my father's burns, just like the parents of the dead girl can't blame me for her death, but I'm angry that she let my father go up onto that roof without a suit. I know he's stubborn, but he would have listened, if she'd tried. I'm in no mood for anything but answers right now.

"Where is *Elaine*?" I whisper, staring at her hard.

She backs up a little. "The girl you were with? She went with you..."

I step away, rake my hands through my hair, suddenly desperate. Elaine didn't come back to the reactor. She wasn't in the hospital. I already checked my apartment. She's gone. Gone and outside without a suit, and a flare could come at any moment, and she said she was safe, protected, but I don't know if that's true—how could it be true? I feel as if don't know anything for certain anymore. Actually, no, I know one thing: that I need to find her.

I walk.

It's almost nightfall, not that that really means anything in Bronze City. The sky gets a little darker, but even when the sun sets, its bulky haze of orange still lies along the horizon. The stars used to be clearer, brighter, but now you can barely make them out. Still, there are a stubborn few.

I've reached my own block, and Elaine is standing right outside of my building. She's got her arms wrapped around her, and her head's tilted back as she stares up at the sky.

"Elaine," I whisper, so weak with relief at having found her that my voice cracks.

She blinks; it takes a moment for her eyes to adjust...to here, now. They were looking for something miles and miles away.

"Maggie," she says simply, and then she stares back up at the sky.

"We should get inside, Elaine. It isn't safe."

"There won't be another flare for a while," she tells me. "I just wanted to see the stars." Her voice is low, thick with a feeling I can't name. "I needed to see them."

I stand silent, watching her with her face tilted up to the pinpricks of stars, as if she's bathing in their light. But the stars are so vague, so distant, they're almost not there. If you're not staring at them hard enough, holding them firm in your sights, they seem to wink out and disappear.

Elaine stares at them fiercely.

"I used to feel so sad," she whispers, "when the stars died. I watched these worlds live and grow. There were so many people on them. There were so many stories, and there were many bad stories, but there were good ones, too. There were moments, watching, that I felt my heart break and ache for people I had never met, would never touch. And then their star blinked out, and in one great, terrible..." She shudders and looks down at the ground, rubbing at her arms absently. "In one terrible moment," she goes on, coughing a little, "so many lives— gone. I was powerless. I made stars, and I made them to last, but no matter what, inevitably, they died. You know," she tells me, wiping a tear from her cheek, "I tried to make a forever star once."

I wait while she adjusts her overalls' suspenders, lying them evenly against her shoulders. She peers up the stars again, hands at her sides. "I called it a forever star because I wanted it to live forever. I made it and remade it and molded it and shaped it. It was supposed to stand until the end of time, until the end of the universe. Longer."

"What happened?" I ask her, but she's already shaking her head.

"It lived the longest of all of my stars, but it died in the end, as they always do. Now I think a forever star is an impossibility. Perhaps there are laws against it, laws I do not know, cannot break. Forever just... It can't be sustained."

We stand for a long time, quiet, looking up. Finally, Elaine sighs and glances at me.

"Thank you," I tell her again, and I think I'll spend the rest of my short life telling her that. "What you did back there—"

She smiles a little, a sad smile, eyes downcast. "In small ways, I can affect the influence of a star, manipulate its outcome. I have power over that. But only that. Even in this body, I can do it. Which is...strange." She looks at her hands, open palms before her. "I didn't know if I could heal him until I tried. I'm glad I could. He's important to you. Do you love him?"

I nod, breathing out. "He's my father. And the best mechanic who ever was. He helped build the reactor."

"A child's love for her father. I saw that, too, on the worlds." She smiles. "Your love for him is admirable."

I bite my lip and stare down at my boots. "It's just how I feel."

She takes a single step, and her shoulder slides against mine, her arm against mine, too, and she reaches for my hand, gently squeezing my fingers.

I can't sleep. I keep thinking about death, and Sarge, and how Elaine's eyes glowed with the brightest light, and every time I shift on the blanket, on the floor, I glimpse her laying still and serene upon the broken couch, hands pillowed beneath her head like the old ads for mattresses.

A universe of emotion churns within me. I'm thinking too much, feeling too much, and I finally sigh, and I thought it was a low sigh, a sigh she couldn't hear, but Elaine opens her eyes in the dark and looks across the space between us. Looks at me.

We don't speak, but we gaze at one another, eyes locked. Slowly, softly, she slides down from the couch, and—on her hands and knees—crawls to me, a little smile lifting the corners of her mouth as her hips sway.

When she kisses me, arcing down like a ray of light, like a gossamer, sacred thing, I reach up to her, wrapping my arms about her ribs, around her heart. I pull her down to me like I've captured a star.

I wake, and Elaine is gone.

She's not in the wash pod; she's not out in the hall. She's not in front of the brick house; and she's not at the reactor. She's not at Sarge's, and she's not in the alley. The panic that engulfs me is surreal, hot, burning. I have to find her. What if this is the last day? It can't end like this, apart. No matter what happens, no matter what, it can't end like this.

Panicked, suitless, I trudge all over the streets and alley, and when I'm too weary to take another step, I see Elaine's shape at the edge of the city, near the gates. The gates used to open and close to the outside world, but they've been sealed shut for as long as I can remember.

Elaine's hand rests against the corroded metal of one of the gates, and she's staring up at the flickering dome in the early morning light.

"It grew," she whispers to me, and I can't see her face here in the shadows, don't understand, but then she's turning to me, and her eyes are filled with tears, and she puts her arms about my neck, and she kisses me. I taste salt in the kiss, and I taste the stuff of stars, and when she pulls away from me, I linger longer, wrapping her tightly in my hug.

"Love grew," she tells me then, explaining, wiping away her tears.

"Yes," I tell her, but what I don't tell her is that I wish we had more time—time to spend together, time to talk and laugh, time to memorize the lines of her palms and the arch of her neck, to figure out which jokes make her laugh and which ones make her frown. I want time to talk to her about history, about civilizations and galaxies, and I want time to tell her, to *show* her how grateful I am to have found her.

The clock ticks in my head, in my heart, even as the rumble begins in the ground beneath our feet: the first sign of a major solar flare.

"The forever star," she whispers to me. "I know what I did wrong now."

I stare at her, hold onto her, even as her body begins to burn and flow with light, as it begins to pulse.

"Don't forget me," she whispers, and she brushes her lips against my cheek.

I open my mouth to speak, but I am drowned in brilliance.

Elaine stood on the edge of the marble balcony, looking down and down into the maelstrom of moons and worlds and stars. She turned, and her sisters sat in their seats, making, hands dripping with the beginnings of matter. Luna looked up, smiled and patted the seat beside her, as if Elaine had never left.

But Elaine had left, and she was changed.

She plucked the dying star out of the sky. She

rolled it in her hands, nurturing it with the warmth of her fingers, the warmth of her heart. And then she drew open the folds of opalescent skin over her ribs, reached within the cage of bones, and plucked out the growing thing, the pulsing thing, the new thing. She added it to the mass of the sun and merged the two together—the star and the bit of herself that would forevermore keep the star alive, so long as Elaine was careful to watch it, so long as Elaine's own heart beat.

And she set the star near the planet, but not too near, and she coaxed it out of her grasp like a shining fish released back into the water. The sun bobbed gently in the blackness until it affixed itself back in place, reformed, reborn.

Elaine watched the life of Maggie Terrence unfold in what amounted—from her lofty seat—to a heartbeat, watched her grow old, watched as new cities were built around her, as the world came alive again. And when Maggie perished, as all mortals do, Elaine did what she had always done: she took that soul and made of it another star, a new star, and set it in a new sky of a new galaxy filled with new worlds.

She watches over that forever star still.

FIN

Sarah Diemer writes about courageous young ladies who love other ladies, makes jewelry out of words and wire and loves her wife more than anything, *ever*. She randomly sparkles.

You can find out about her novels, novellas and short stories, take a peek at the jewelry she makes out of old fairy tales and generally see several sparkly and interesting things at her site, http://www.oceanid.org, or the blog she shares with her wife at, http://www.muserising.com She also writes magical lesbian love stories under the pen name "Elora Bishop"—you can find out more here: http://elorabishop.wordpress.com

Connect with the author at:
http://twitter.com/sarahdiemer
Facebook search: **Sarah Diemer, Author**

Please sign up for the author's newsletter at Oceanid.org
or http://eepurl.com/h6KF2
You'll be the first one to know about Sarah's new releases!

22292583R00111

Made in the USA
Lexington, KY
24 April 2013